MASOCHIST

....

Jennifer Preston

Contents

----

1. Popcorn.   1

2. Found u.   7

3. Blood.   13

4. Little bunny.   19

5. Doll.   25

6. Brat   30

7. You cant do this.   36

8. Promises   45

9. normal?   54

10. misunderstanding   60

11. Safe place.   68

12. Freedom.   73

13. Disrepect.   79

14. Confusion.   85

15. Pills.   90

16. Masquerade.   95

17. Our fun.   100

18. Aftermath.   106

19. A game?   112

20. Let the games begin.   116

21. Was it so simple?   121

22. West wing.   126

23. Dumbfounded.   131

24. Nothing gets me excited like, you.   137

25. Soft.   142

26. Memories.   147

Popcorn.

E velyn.

I slipped on my white night gown, Victoria already put on her black one she went downstairs to grab some popcorn so we can finally watch this movie we've been planning for a week.

I've been super busy with my job and she's been very busy with hers. But we finally have time. Normally when we have off days I stay with her, she has a huge house and her family is never home. She lives alone. She got the house after her parents died when she was 18 she's 22 now, we have 3 years between us but it doesn't affect our friendship. I've always been very mature for my age.

I laid under the warm fuzzy blanket while I scrolled through the movie list. She wants to watch a horror movie very bad. Seeing as the house is in the middle of no where it scares the shit out of me but she really wants it.

I jumped as she threw the door open. "Jesus vic." I grabbed my heart seeing a grin on her face she walked over to the bed with the two bags of popcorn.

We decided on Insidious.

~

Half way through the movie my mouth felt dry and I needed a drink. "Hey are you thirsty?" I asked vic who was laying with her head on my shoulder munching on popcorn. She made a soft mhm sound. I slipped away letting her head fall to the pillow while walking downstairs.

I bit my lip, the cold air and stone floors make my nipples cold. It hurts.

I walked down the cold steps all the way to the huge kitchen. I live in a 2 bedroom one bathroom apartment, I've been keeping up a waitress job to keep my apartment and be able to eat etc.

I grabbed a glass out the cupboard. The big window had sheer fabric over it, a red light showed through them my eyebrows furrowed setting the glass down and moving the blindes.

"A car?" I stared at it for a bit watching it park in confusion. No one ever comes here...

I walked up the steps halfway up I heard a loud roaring sound like a motor. My heart jumped i ran upstairs, seeing vic already in the door way eyes wide. I knew something was off.

Who are these people?

"Evelyn get in dont come out" she shoved me in the room and closed the door. I fell on my butt eyes wide and my jaw dropped I got up adjusting my dress. Vic has these huge windows that go from floor to the ceiling.

I open the blindes slightly seeing all the lights off on the car and a figure taking off its helmet while sitting on a motorcycle still.

My jaw dropped seeing two large, and I mean huge. Figures move out of the car and walk towards the front door.

Who are these people.

The door heard a loud banging before I heard it shut again. All the people now inside.

I put my hand on the wall and the door carefully opening it trying to make no sound. I slowly walked over to the stairs where they have a half wall going down the staircase. I softly moved up trying to look over it.

"What are you doing here" vic said with her hands covering her body. not her normal confident voice. She sounded shaky. Caught of guard. "Ew put on some fucking clothes" one scoffed.

"Right. And It's my house sis" I heard someone say another chuckling. "Why? You don't like us visiting to see how you're doing?" I heard another male speak up.

"You're not here for me" she said moving back. "You're right. We need the house for the week, i dont care where u stay. Its not here. You have 10 minutes to pack your shit" the first one spoke up again.

My eyes widened.

She stumbled back obviously stunned, ever since I've known her she's been in this house and no one ever visits. Not on holidays. Not on birthdays. Never.

"N-no i stay here!" She spoke up. One male walked forward but another held up his hand stopping his movement. "5 minutes. Now Victoria." The sternness in his voice made my heart drop.

Vic stumbled back before running up the stairs I quickly ran back to her room before she could see me. She came in crying her eyes already red. I hugged her quickly trying to calm her down. "It's not fair!" She hugged my shoulders while crying on one.

"I don't have long" she quickly broke the hug grabbing a big sport bag and frantically packing clothes and everything she needed.

After five minutes she put a normal outfit on. "You cant come with me, they're murderers Evelyn, they'll take you. You have to hide. Now." She stressfully told me.

"Hide in here they dont come in my room, stay quiet try sneak out at midnight or tomorrow and be really careful" she said my eyes wide from her previous statement but shaking my head. She quickly rushed out not wanting them to come and get her and find me. I quickly rushed over to the door to lock it.

I could hear faint talking but not much I looked through the blindes the dark night still early, I watched her get in her car.

~

I laid down in the sheets trying to calm my heart beat. I've heard them walk around. Sometimes closely to the room im in other time they talk upstairs. Its driving me insane.

I close my eyes trying to drift off to sleep before hearing a voice in the hall. "Hey Elias come here real quick."

I closed my eyes shut trying not to hear anything. A loud "Hm?" Rang through the hall. "Who's car is that?" My heart sank. No.

I'm going to die.

They're going to kill me.

I quickly looked for a window, but none open and the ones that do, there's no way I can jump down its way to far up.

Before I could think the door nob twisted but it didn't open a frustrated bang hit the door. "What the fuck?" I heard a voice say.

"Why is it locked?" He seemed to be thinking out loud. "Here." One spoke up. I didn't hear anything. I quickly hid under the bed all the way in the corner rolled up in a ball.

I closed my eyes a loud bang hitting the door out of place and onto the floor. I gulped trying to hold back tears.

they're murderers Evelyn.they're murderers Evelyn.they're murderers Evelyn.

I saw two pair of shoes enter first then another. A soft "hm" was all that was said. "Is she hiding something?" He thought out loud. "Ill find it." I could hear the smirk in his voice.

The shoes first walked to the bathroom throwing the door open. I flinched from the door hitting the stone wall probably denting it.

The other footsteps sat on the bed the end of their feet facing me. I gulped trying to control my breathing but it seemed impossible.

"She's definitely hiding something." He came out again walking around the room and throwing the wardrobe open. Aggressive ripping clothes out and throwing them everywhere he laid on the ground with his ear while tapping on it with his fingers.

"Did she put it in the floor?" I moved back a sharp edge of the bed pressing into my back causing me to softly yelp. His face shot up his ear still to the ground now looking at me with a crazy look in his eyes and the most terrifying smirk I've ever seen.

Found u.

E velyn
"Gotcha" he smiled before quickly crawling over to me and trying to grab my ankle, I began kicking against his hands a more angry expression moved over his face my eyes filled with tears.

they're murderers Evelyn.

My head couldn't stop repeating what Victoria said.

"Come on, dont be scared" he finally grabbed onto one of my ankles pulling me from under the bed my hands scraped over the floor trying to grab onto something but he yanked me from under the bed.

"I knew she was hiding something." He grabbed my hair his hand holding onto my scalp tilting my head backwards to look into his eyes. "Now, who may you be." He smirked amusement filling his eyes as tears strained my cheeks.

A hand wrapped around my waist lifting my feet up from the ground. "LET ME GO!" I quickly began struggling again trying to get out of his grip but even tho he only held me with one arm, I was no match.

He carried me downstairs as if I weight nothing. "Look what I caught Elijah." he put me down finally i quickly covered my body seeing the male smirk.

"Who are you?" He bend down to my eye level with his hands in his pockets his breath on my lips. I tried backing off but I moved into the other males figure.

"Evelyn...." I looked down trying to avoid eye contact the other guy also came downstairs sitting on the couch. "Evelyn." He looked up at the guy behind me.

"How old are you Evelyn." I looked up taking in his features, a eyebrow piercing on his left eyebrow. When he spoke something shined in his mouth.

"Nineteen" I bit the inside of my cheek growing nervous as he smirked again. He stood up putting his hand on my jaw and face, he forced me to look at him.

I realised he had tattoos in his neck and on his arm. A shiver ran down my spine causing the male behind me to chuckle. "Why would Victoria leave u over to us hm?" He didn't let me answer. It wasn't a question.

He's mocking the fact he has me.

Before I could answer his lips crashed into mine I pushed at his shoulders trying to move him out of my way but two hands grabbed ahold of my upper arm forcing my arms behind me. I dropped to my knees but I couldn't. He lift me up not letting me move.

Second person.

Elijahs hand snakes up to her breast pinching it letting him enter his tongue into her mouth. He let out a satisfied 'hm' once she yelped and finally opened her jaws allowing his tongue to explore her mouth.

Her struggling only made him want her more. He pulled away letting her breathe. "We're going to have so much fun darling" his hand grabbed ahold of her face making her look up at him. "I like this toy." He spoke to his brother who nod in agreement. "My turn." Theodore spoke up a massive grin on his face when the female starts to struggle again.

"Please! Let me go-" before she could finish her sentence he turned her around still holding her arms behind her back and smashed his lips onto hers causing her eyes to fill with tears. She had one ex, one.

That was enough for her not to want a sexual experience ever again, it wasn't the fact he came in less then five seconds, it was the fact he thought she did too.

She had always fantasised about the sex books talk about. The sparkling feeling. The carving. The ropes. To have someone who would never let her go, simply because they wouldn't be able to live without her.

Now being in the arms of three bigger men she feared every single one of those thoughts.

After biting her tongue to make her yelp in pain he finally let her catch air which she did in a panick not having enough air from his hand choking her.

"A-are y-you going to k-kill m-e?" Theodore furrowed a brow and looked at his brother who shrug. They both glanced over to Elias who was enjoying the scene from the couch. "Lets keep her." Elijah said fear ripped through her. He finally put her down but she didn't dare move. She didn't bother covering herself not wanting to make them angry.

"Fun little toy." Elijah grabbed her lifting her off the ground her mind went blank realising she was over his shoulder. She scratched at his back not knowing it turns him on even more.

"You should be happy we're not killing you, you seem sad almost." She didn't answer not seeing a point. He threw her down on a large bed. One way too big for one person, two even. There could fit 4 people in this bed it looked like.

Her dress moved up slightly revealing her thighs and her stomach, but most important to Elijah, her white laced panties.

A smirk grew onto his lips terrifying her. Shortly after the other two followed behind, Elias sitting next to her face caressing her hair. She flinched at first but didn't say anything. A small smile grew onto his lips.

Theodore stood on the other side of the bed. She could feel her panties slip off. "NO." She screamed protesting she started kicking and hitting.

She got confused feeling a cold something on her face. She stopped moving opening one eye.

Her eyes widened seeing Theodore point a gun at the side of her temple. "Looks like we're going to have to train you." Elijah said she could see the annoyance over his face. Her bottom lip trembled feeling the barrel against her face.

Elijah slipped her panties off displaying her cunt on display for him. He licked his lips looking at her feared eyes made his cock drip with desire.

He spread her legs easily even tho she tried her hardest to keep them shut she was no match for him. Or any of them for that matter.

He licked her slit hearing her breath hitch he smiled. "So sensitive" he blew cold air onto her bud. A whimper left her lips. Theo could feel his length stir with desire.

He gave her a couple more annoying licks before latching onto her bud and sucking onto it harshly. "N-ah please s-sto-ah" she tried to talk but only moans were heard.

Before she could even clear her mind Elias began sucking on her neck causing big purple hickeys to form. Theo smirked moving the sheer fabric off her already hard nipple. He flicked his finger making her half moan from Elijah and half yell from Theo.

He licked her nipple coating it with saliva. She didn't know how to protest anymore with all the pleasure she felt. And she felt horrible for thinking it felt nice.

His tongue slit in and out of her entrance. The pinching at one nipple and the licking at the other send her over edge sending her into a long tiring orgasm. She closed her eyes tired.

Elias didn't get off. Theo didnt. And neither did Elijah. Her eyes opened again tiredly trying to move away. But she was no match awake. Sleeping they didn't even have to try.

"Sleepy so quick? Never had a orgasm have u baby" Theo taunted in her ear causing her to groan. "Awww you haven't" he teased squeezing her nipple.

Elijah continued to fuck her with his tongue while moving his thumb over her saliva coated bud sending her over the edge soon after the last.

"Nono pls pls" she begged squirming around. "Hm.. maybe if you beg properly." Elijah said before going back to circling his tongue around her clit.

"Please elija-ah-" she felt another orgasm rip through her tiring her even more. "Hm?" He continued.

"Plea-se El-ij-ah" she tried to speak. "Call me Daddy." He demanded. Her head was so far in the clouds she didn't even care. She couldn't think anymore. She never actually had a orgasm.

She didn't think it really existed.

But they proofed her wrong.

"Pleas-E da-ddy.." she moaned in her high voice from being Send over the edge too much. "There we go angel" he kissed her flit before putting her panties back on. "You can sleep in your cum like our filthy little slut." He pressed his thumb onto her cunt one more time after the panties were on making her moan from being too sensitive.

"I cant wait to fuck you brains out" Theo whispered.

Blood.

E velyn

    I opened my eyes feeling something heavy. Elijah on my legs with his head and his arms. Someone on my stomach(Theo) with his head. And someone (Elias) holding onto my arm.

I tried to move but they're so heavy. "Go back to sleep." The one on my stomach groaned. I furrowed my brows. "I don't want to sleep." He opened his eyes. "Go to sleep Evelyn, before I fuck you to sleep." I gulped quickly closing my eyes and drifting off to sleep.

A couple hours later I woke up all alone.

How did I not notice three massive men leaving the bed...?

I got up looking in the giant mirror that's on the door. I gulped seeing red bruises and bite marks on my neck and bruises on my breast. I softly opened the door making sure it doesn't make a sound i top toed to Victoria's room. She will have something more appropriate to wear.

"Where do you think you're going?" My eyes sprung wide open. I stopped in my tracks turning around to seeing the guy who captured me.

"Uh.. well..." I looked down at my outfit. "I thought I would change into something more.. well appropriate..."

"Why? This is perfect." He said looking down at my dress causing me to try cover myself.

Before I could even cover myself he slammed me into the hall wall. Taking my hands off my chest and putting them above my head I stared at him wide eyed. "Did I tell you to fucking cover yourself?" I shook no my breath hitching. "Then I struggle to find a reason why U did." I looked at him shaking.

"If you wanna live. You're gonna fucking listen Evelyn." He grabbed my jaw, kissing my forehead and backing off again leaving me still stuck in my position. "I think this is fine. Come downstairs and eat." He walked down the stairs without another word.

My mind went blank following him not wanting to piss anyone off I stumbled behind him to the dining room. I knew victorias family was a bit well, complicated she always said. She never said her brothers are psychos or that she has three.

I guess there's lot I didn't know about her.

I sat down in the middle of the table the guy who caught me infront and the other two on both heads of the table.

"No Goodmorning kiss?" Elijah spoke up. My eyes widened. I slowly shook my head seeing the other guys fist slam the table and walking towards me I began shaking hiding myself as Best as I could.

"Leave her." The other of which I didn't know his name spoke up. He scooped me up in his arms as if I didn't weigh anything and put me down in his lap.

I can already tell he's the most gentle with the way he caressed my hair and is now moving his thumb over my back trying to calm me down. "Here." He spoke up grabbing the fork my head laid against his chest in a ball. He did something making a scraping sound and bringing it to my mouth. I could see ring on his fingers and a small tattoo by his wrist.

I opened my mouth and took a bite scolding myself for obeying them. After the plate was done he pulled my chin up to look at him. His thumb swiped the side of my lip taking away any access food.

"Thank u.." I softly whispered seeing a small smile appear on his face. "Of course love." He let me sit up normal but he wrapped his arms around my waist when I tried to hop off. My feet dangled above the floor not being able to reach it on his lap.

"Now Evelyn." Elijah spoke up making me gulp again. "You know my name right?" I nod. "What's my name?"

"Elijah.." I mumbled. "Hm?" He spoke up wanting me to say it harder. "Elijah .." I spoke up. "Wrong." I looked up confused. "What did I tell you yesterday?" I thought for a moment trying to relive the evening with how fuzzy my head was at the end.

"Daddy...." I whispered. A smirk grew on his lips. "There we go." He proceeded to walk over to me and grab me out of the other persons arms. Before sitting down next to him and putting me on his own lap. The other male walked around the table too.

Me now sitting between both them on elijahs lap definitely makes me nervous. "Do you know what u call Theo?" I shook my head feeling a shiver go down my spine by his deep voice near my ear.

"You can call me master, kitten." He grabbed my chin making me face him I gulped nodding. He raised a brow showing me I had to say it.

"Master...." I whispered embarrassed looking down. "There we go, such a innocent little lamb." He smirked.

"Now Elias, u can call sir." He whispered i nod. I felt a slight pinch in my waist I whined before saying "Sir.."

"There we go, now how about we have some fun huh?" He flipped me around and lifted my ass onto the table.

Second person.

She sat on the table seeing Theo, Elijah, and Elias sit below her grew her more nervous with the minute. Elijah slipped off her panties and Theo stuffed them in his pocket with a smirk.

"No please-" she tried it resist but he already plunged his finger into her making her moan in a way she never had before. He smirked finding her sweet spot so easily. "Come on baby, you're enjoying it. Be a good little slut." He rubbed his thumb over her clit causing her to lay down unable to sit up from the pleasure. Before she could even get her mind straight Theo latched onto her stomach creating big purple hickeys and Elias decided to take a pretty picture of them for if she ever disobeys.

Elias wasn't as harsh as his brothers, he could be. But only if u disobey him. Other then that he's very calm and nice. Except for the fact he would love to cut her up. Carve his name into her thigh, collar bone, waist. Anywhere. And slowly watch the blood drop down her gorgeous soft skin.

He knew where this was going the minute they saw the small petite girl. The way she shakes or shivers. How she looks up with her big green eyes and how her soft brown/blonde hair waves down to her ass.

The way her collar bones stuck out and the way her cheeks are big enough for you to want to squeeze her face like a cat.

She was their ideal imagine.

Elias couldn't control himself anymore seeing her head throw back and lifting her back up slightly he needed to carve something into her.

He grabbed his pocket knife out of his pocket growing more and more possessive he knew the perfect spot.

He waited for Elijah to get her near her orgasm and when he did. The blade pressed below her boob on her ribs drawing blood out of it.

She didn't even notice which made him love it even more. After a long exhausting orgasm he finally wrote Elias on her stomach.

Evelyn

I whispered feeling myself come down from yet another exhausting orgasm, I can feel something sting but it's probably one of them biting meI opened my eyes getting dizzy Elias grabbed onto my back steadying me before Elijah picked me up and put me on the floor. I almost fell if it wasn't for Elias picking me up.

"I think its bath time for you" he picked me up and carried me upstairs to one of the bathrooms. My head laid against his chest hearing his heartbeat calms me down for some reason.

He put me on the toilet while filling the sink and grabbing a aid box out of the cabinets.

I furrowed my brows. Why does he need that?

Before I could say anything he slipped the dress over my head leaving me in my lingerie.

I shook the cold air hitting me.

"Here stay still it will sting a little." He dabbed a Cotten ball on my rib causing me to flinch and look st it. E l I A S.

My eyes widened seeing his name on me. "U carved your name into me?..." I stood up backing off I could see a panick in his eyes.

"I uh.." I looked down at it and began running before I could even take two steps I was lifted into the air I kicked and screamed but it was no use. Before I could even think of my next move the other two were here too.

"LETS ME GOO" i shouted scratching at his arms. "IM NOT SOMR TOY LET ME GO!" I shouted trying to get out of his grip.

"You're our fucking toy." Theo spoke up.

Little bunny.

E velyn.

"Evelyn." Elijah shouted, i dont care. I clawed at Elias's arms wanting to get out of his grip and out of this house. I'm not theirs. I need to get away. I don't know why they wont let me go or just kill me.

I furrowed my brows feeling someone press fabric on my mouth before I could shout I began feeling dizzy.

"What.." my eyes fell halfway down, I couldn't scratch him anymore because my arms wouldn't move. "Le-t m-e go.."

Everything went black.

~

I woke up in a white room, everything is white from the sheets to the walls to the light that's coming into the room all the way down to the carpet.

I sat up trying to remember what happened. "Did they drug me?..." i whisper looking down. Then at my clothes.

Panic shoots through me when I see I'm not wearing the clothes I was wearing before.

My eyes widen seeing Elijah walk in. I crawl back in the bed hearing a chuckle from him.

"Sweetheart, me and Elias have to do something, I need you to be a good girl and listen to Theo can u do that?" I bit my lip slowly nodding. This is my chance to get away. I can get away from one but not three..

"If you don't you only got yourself with it, he's not very happy when ppl disobey him." He tucked his blouse into his pants before throwing his blazer over his shoulders.

He looks hot.

No he doesn't, shut up Evelyn.

I nod as he explained him and Elias we're only going to be away for the day.

"Make daddy proud and listen." He pulled my jaw up kissing me my hands on his chest trying to push him away but it's no use. He wont move.

I could feel him getting horny by the way he's pressing me into the pillow laying half on me.

"Hey, hey, hey, that's mine for today" Theo walks in I can hear a chuckle from Elijah as he finally pulls away giving me on more kiss before actually getting up. "Trying to devour my desert" he rolled his eyes laying next to me with his hand under his head supported by his elbow.

"So what u in the mood for princess?" I shrugged. "Does that involve going ho-"

"This is your fucking home Evelyn. Where we are, Is ur home." His jaw tightened. Clearly annoyed. I looked away.

"I'll show some other way then." He ripped the covers off trailing his hands down my body i squirmed around trying to come free but I couldn't.

"Oh really?" He mocked me.

I give up.

Laying there still trying to make this go as fast as it possibly could. My brows knotted feeling his finger enter me.

He looked at me puzzled until he spoke up "you've never even?" He seemed joyful, as if he just won the jackpot. "So you're telling me, your little cunt is a virgin?" I gulped but nod not wanting to have him make me say it.

He chuckled grinning. "We're never letting you go. You do know that right?" My eyes widened. I will. I just need to come up with a plan. I nod slowly a tear falling down my cheek he licked it up making me turn my face away.

He didn't say anything. Instead he started pumping his finger in and out of me coating it with wetness making me grow even more embarrassed.

My moans we're uncontrollable making my cheeks cost a soft red colour.

I grabbed ahold of his wrist trying to slow his fingers down but he only moved faster placing his thumb over my clit I gave up and laid my head down in the pillow.

I felt a sting in my thigh. Too focused by my upcoming orgasm I couldn't exactly guess what it was.

Before I could move away little lightening sparks flew all over my body as the orgasm finally hit me.

"Not very polite are you slut. Say thank you." He kissed the crook of my neck. I whispered, "thank you.." a groan could be heard coming from him. A very annoyed one might I add.

"Call me by my name." he seemed annoyed. i furrowed my brows. "Think." suddenly i remember the conversation he told me to call him master.. a spark lights up in his eyes realising i know.

I nod slowly. "Thank you Master.." I gulped a big grin plastered across his face made me more anxious then it should've.

"Do you want something to eat?" He asked sitting up at the edge of the bed. I nod. I need food in me before I try and run away.

He put his hand out gesturing me to grab and without any choice I did.

We walked downstairs i frantically let go of his hand when i finally saw milo. I could hear a chuckle coming from him as I picked the fuzzy grey cat up.

"Milo seems to love you" he said walking into the kitchen hearing the cat pur instantly as I picked it up.

"Don't tell Victoria.. but he's a big reason I come here" i said sitting on the chair near the kitchen island scratching behind the cats ears.

"I wont." I could see a small smile form on his face. When he acts like this he's kinda.. normal?

Because he wasn't wearing a shirt the snake tattoo on his back was visible. Victoria had a little snake on her wrist.

"Is it a family tattoo..?" I said slowly referring to the tattoo. His back seemed to tense for a second but then let go again as he turned around and leaned onto the kitchen counter.

A smirk appeared on his lips, "it's funny you ask that, maybe you'll listen then." It seemed like he had gotten an idea.

"Are you familiar with Victoria's last name?" I furrowed my brows. Why's that important?

"Uh she told me i think but I don't remember.." I said confused on how it's relevant.

"It isn't exactly a family tattoo, but I'll give you my last name darling, Everest" a small smirk appeared on his lips.

"I've heard of it before but I don't know it" I shrugged watching him shake his head and smile. "Look it up darling." he turned around again.

They haven't restricted any internet, my phone is still in Victoria's room I could call police and get out??

I smiled feeling a plan come up in me I looked down at milo. "What's making u so happy" he said cooking up some eggs.

"Nothing." I smiled. "Adres me properly." He deadpanned coming closer. I gulped. "Nothing master.." I bit the inside of my cheek seeing a glinstering satisfaction in his eyes.

He kissed me before turning back to the eggs. "Do you think I could go to the bathroom?.. master.." I gulped again trying to get it out. He smiled nodding. I hopped off the seat putting the cat down and walking upstairs.

The cold floor make me even more anxious as I ran over towards Victoria's room. I looked under the pillow smiling.

My phone.

I guilty put it in the back of my panties as I didn't have any pants and ran over to the bathroom.

But before I could attempt to get up. I felt a large figure creep over me. "Why would u use Victoria's bathroom dear, you know we have one downstairs." He grabbed the back of my neck lifting me up. I squealed trying to get his hand off me. He was still wearing his cooking apron.

"Something tells me you weren't looking for the bathroom darling." His face inched closer to mine I shut my eyes tilting my head as much as I could with his grip.

"Was my little bunny trying to escape?" He whispered against my ear sending a shiver down my spine.

Doll.

E velyn.

"Answer me Evelyn." I opened my eyes realising what would happen if he found out about my phone.

I gulped. "No.. I wasn't." I whispered. "You know you can't right?" I could feel tears prickle in my eyes. "Right." He insisted annoyed.

"You know, I'm not very fucking patient, and im really running out of patience love." I bit my lip to stop it from trembling. "I-im s-sorry m-mas-ter the-o" A tear fel down my cheek. He licked it up kissing along my cheek.

"You're never gonna escape." He put me down on my feet. "Because if you try," he smiled and reached to the side of his pants.

A gun.

My heart skipped a beat hearing Victoria.

They're killers ...

Tears fell down my cheeks. "I'll kill you. No one else if having you." He caressed my hair with his other hand putting the gun back in his pants and grabbing my hand in his almost crushing it.

He dragged me through the hall his legs being much taller then mine made me stumble multiple times. He sighed deeply before picking me up annoyed with my stumbling.

I can feel my heart hammer against my chest. As soon as I'm alone I need to call the police.

"Uh how late is eli-" his eyes shot down. I gulped down any self worth I had knowing that's not what I'm supposed to call him. "How late are the others home.." I tried rephrasing it.

"Hm." He looked on his watch carrying me down the stairs. "About an hour." He kept walking till we reached the kitchen. He put me down now sitting on the kitchen island. The eggs were done in a bowl next to the stove. There were pancakes and a smoothie.

How the hell did he do all that and still catch me so fast?

He turned around grabbing the bowl with eggs and a fork before forcing some of it in my mouth i chewed on it, not too moist not too dry. At least he can cook.

"Good?" He asked i nod still chewing he seemed satisfied with himself before pushing more into my mouth and cutting the pancakes pouring syrup over it and some cut strawberries.

He also forced that in not letting me eat anything or at my own pace almost choking. He definitely doesn't have a lot of patience.

I managed to get everything down plus the smoothie which would normally be way too much food for me but I didn't have much of a choice with him forcing it in.

"Time to shower." My eyes widened. "Uh actually i was wondering if uh if we could watch a movie!" I said trying to not get undressed and have him find the phone.

He furrowed his brows but agreed "Alright then." He carried me off the counter, I prayed to god the phone wouldn't slip out and that he wouldn't feel it with the way he held my under my arms and under my knees.

He laid me down on the couch. "I actually really have to pee.." I said looking down. "But i thought u went to use the bathroom earlier?" I bit my lip. "I didn't get to it because u scared me.."

He sighed. "Fine let's go." He said taking my hand I gulped he's not gonna come in right.

I opened the door walking in feeling him walk in behind me i quickly stopped turning around. "Please.. it's humiliating having someone be there when u go to the toilet..." I gulped. I know I shouldn't disobey him but please.

He checked the bathroom probably for windows but there are nun. He nod letting me walk in by myself. I quickly took the phone out and threw it very far behind in a drawer. I flushed the toilet and washed my hands to make it seem like I actually used it.

He leaned against the wall on his phone ticking away aggressively. I moved back on the front and back of my feet a couple times before he took my hand again and walked with me to the cinema in the house. Normally me and Victoria just used her tv in her room.

He moved his phone to his head. "Be quiet will you." He said sternly. I nod slowly.

"Get it fucking done I told you two fucking days ago and you're still busy? You're fucking useless." He hung up and put it on silent in his pocket annoyed.

He turned to me now smiling. "Im sorry for that doll." He kissed me before getting up. "I'll get some popcorn you can put on a movie okay?" I nod watching him disappear.

I looked on the clock. I have less then 30 mins before the others are back if they are here I have no chance in getting the phone.

If I try escape I get killed ...

I ran towards the bathroom full speed trying to not get seen by him or get caught.

My feet ran faster then I could keep up luckily it's only one hall further. I sucked in a quick breath before quickly diving in the drawer and grabbing the phone. I shacking typed in 911.

It takes about 2 minutes to make popcorn. Running took me one.

"My name is Evelyn Blaine, Im being kidnapped they wont let me go and they have a gun they will kill me uh i believe they're last name is uhhh" I thought rlly hard and finally got it. "Everest!" I quickly threw the phone back in the drawer seeing the clock i couldnt say anything else. Out of panic I forgot the address even tho Victoria mostly drove me here. Hoping they will track the call since it was still calling its my only hope.

I quickly ran back trying to catch my breath I saw he wasn't back yet I sat down trying to collect my breathing but it wouldn't calm down with the intense fear of him finding out.

What if he shoots me in the head. Right now.

I saw him coming back with what looked like a bucket of popcorn and a large drink with two straws.

He put the bucket on the table infront before grabbing a blanket and sitting down himself.

"So what movie is it going to be dolly."

Brat

E velyn.

"Uhh... titanic?" I said the first thing that came up in my mind. "Fine with me doll." He grabbed the remote and put the movie on, his arm wrapped around my waist moving me towards him.

"Your heart is beating crazy." He said his face nuzzling into my neck. "Are you nervous?" He has pressed a soft slow kiss against my neck. I flinched the front door slamming closed.

"No fair." He got up and walking towards I assume Elijah and Elias.

"Your home too early." He said echoing through the halls. "Yeah well since the idiot you choose didnt do his work right Elias did it for him, so off early." I heard keys smack on a table. "Where is she." I heard Elias say.

I slowly decided to creep along the corner of the hall seeing them all standing. I flinched hearing knocking on the door.

My heart began hammering against my chest again.

Am I free?

Elijah opened the door Theo and Elias clearly confused.

"Uh- mister Everest?" The person spoke my heart sunk.

What.

"Why are you here? We haven't called u in?" He spoke also confused. "Uh there was a call from a person in the house.. it sounded very panicked but we didn't know it was you sir.." he said trembling.

"Go home." He closed the door I flinched again taking a different turn in the hall.

I need to get out.

"Evelyn." Elijah shouted, it echoed through every hall making me worry where he is. "Im going to give u five second to come out, trust me you don't want the punishment darling." I quickly picked up my pace opening every passing by door I could but nun opened. Every window was locked. Everything is locked I ran and ran but there was no out was.

My eyes began getting blurry from tears before falling to the ground.

A chuckle above me.

"You know, I do love a good hunt." Elias stood above me with a knife. My heart sunk once again.

He grabbed the back of my head. A hand full of my hair. He almost dragged me above the ground back to the center of the house. Theo clenched his jaw annoyed. Elijah didnt look much different. Elias on the other hand looked infatuated. Like he won the best thing ever.

He thrives for the hunt. A knife pressed against my neck told me all I needed to know.

"You're killing me arent u.." I felt tears fall down my cheeks.

A collective chuckle from all.

"You think you're getting away that easily? Oh baby. You're ours. Why cant you understand that?" Elijah came closer his thumb caressing my now tear streaming down cheeks.

"If only it was that simple for you hm? Then you got something out of all this disobeying." Fake sympathy laced his voice. "Now we're just going to fuck the disobedience out of you."

"J-just k-kill m-e" I choked out. Elias let me go. Elijahs hand snakes around my waist. His hand a firm grip on my jaw keeping my head up looking at him.

"What did I just tell you? You're ours. You're not getting killed, the only way you'll feel pain is by our hands." He looked at Elias before looking down at me.

"I thought you were actually doing better todsy dolly, I guess not." Theo spoke sitting on the edge of the couch.

I looked down almost feeling bad in his disappointment.

Why do I feel bad?

"You know you're getting punished right baby?" Elijah sternly regained my attention. I gulped. I want to look away but I know it's only going to make it worse. I nod.

"So what would u rather have as a punishment? Your hole fucked or..." he paused looking at Elias before back at me. "What about your pretty mouth?" He gave me a evil smile.

"You decide." His hand moving from my jaw to my neck gripping onto it firmly, cutting off some of my air. My eyes begin getting glossy.

I look at his piercing. His brown eyes that can literally blow a hole through my head.

He clenches his jaw. "Today dear." I gulp again shaking my head. His tongue poked his cheek before he let me go and two hands landed around my waist. Turning me around my back now facing Elijah's front.

My front facing Elias who's holding me so I don't fall over.

And I thought he was the most normal one.

He pressed a hand on my back pushing me forward — bending me over. "Then I decide." My dress flew up right above my ass. And I could feel my underwear rip apart. I gasped feeling the cold air hit my cunt.

Elias grabbed my hair in one hand in a ponytail. I looked up at him, the cold steal of his knife under my throat I could feel a large object being pushed into me I closed my eyes painfully.

Tears streaming down my eyes, "almost darling." His hands were on my waist pushing me backwards he pushed his whole length into me.

I whimpered in pain. "It's okay baby you're going to be screaming in pleasure in a minute." He began moving his hips back and forth making me feel a weird sensation in my tummy.

I opened my eyes seeing Elias's dick now at the tip of my lips. I gulped. "Should've chosen baby." Elias pressed his member into my mouth. I opened feeling the knife press more against my neck.

Elijah's pace sped up sending little electric shocks towards my clit.

My brows knit feeling something built up inside me. I put my hands on Elias's thighs for support.

I moaned feeling a type of pleasure rip through me I've never felt before.

"Ah- go on baby." Elias groaned grabbing onto my hair, he started fucking my throat relentlessly.

Elijah grabbed both my arms bringing them behind my back and holding them to thrust faster.

Groans were heard from both. Elijah's hand landed a hard smack on my ass causing me to moan onto Elias who groaned releasing down my throat.

Soon after Elijah also came not letting a single drop fall out as he picked me up by my waist bounding me up and down on his dick.

"Isn't she a cute fuck toy." He chuckled into my ear. My legs feel numb. I cant collect a single thought.

Elias came closer moving his knife over my nipples. I whimpered at the cold steel. His thumb circled around my clit sending another wave of pleasure into my entire body.

His tongue circled around my nipple. I tried pushing him away but my arms feel like jelly it's no use.

I could feel Elijah getting close again and so was I. Theo stood behind Elias taking a picture but I was too fuzzy to even remember as Elias send me over the edge. And Elijah send another sticky mess down my legs.

I groaned feeling my legs numb.

"Now you wont be able to walk away dolly."

-Theo

You cant do this.

E velyn.

   I couldn't hold my tears back as Elijah's hand ran over my back again. The warm water touching my skin. The soap remaining on most of my body to try and cover myself. It didn't help. His large hands kept throwing water over me.

He groaned in my neck. He disapproved. He doesnt like to use much words, it makes him angry. I let my body relax by stop trying to cover myself.

A kiss on my neck. If approval? Maybe if I just pretend to listen to them I'll get some freedom to get away? I slightly smiled at the thought.

Even tho My last plan didn't work, I still have hope.

His hand moved over my waist to my stomach covering my whole stomach with just one of his hands. I bit my lip looking away. "What dear?" He circled his index finger over my stomach.

What is wrong with me.

"Hm?" he hummed in my ear. I gulped trying to regain my thoughts. "You know I find it disobeying when you don't tell me your thoughts right?" I looked straight ahead, he is very odd. Why does he even care?

"I am not thinking about anything." I slightly gasped as I felt his nails in my back. But not long or bitten nor uncared for nails. They were all very well hygienic in any and every way. Down to their nails, eyebrows and hair.

"Was that a lie?" His head rested on my shoulder. "I'll let you go this once." He kissed my cheek while grabbing me underneath my arms and grabbing me out of the bath.

He's letting me off?

Before he grabbed a towel for himself he got me one and wrapped it around my shoulders. He threw one on my head too, made a indescribable confused face before picking it up and laying it around my shoulders for later.

He wrapped a towel around his waist. I really need to get a grip. His hair dripping wet onto his abs. Its not like I've never noticed how handsome they are. And maybe if we met in a normal situation it would've been fine? But I cant. I need to get away.

I'm horrible for even thinking this.

"Evelyn?" I slightly jumped. "Huh" I looked At Elijah who was holding my shoulders. "Are you okay you zoned out I think" his brows were furrowed. A questioning tone in his voice. "Uh im sorry." I apologised looking down.

"It's okay sweetheart." He seemed to give me what looked like a small smile. I shook my head before feeling his hands on my shoulders again leading me to his room.

I waddled over the floor trying not to slip. It didn't help that he walks much faster and keeps pushing me.

He grabbed me again putting me on his bed. I furrowed my brows. "I have legs." I mumbled. He chuckled, "you're just perfect grabbing size i like carrying you around." He put me down giving me a shrug, before grabbing the towel around my neck and roughly messing up my hair with it.

"Hey hey hey!" I threw my hands up trying to grab the towel. "I'm trying it." He said sternly I quickly put my hands down. He stopped putting it down. "U are cute when you obey." He kissed me before using the same towel on his hair.

"Here" he got one of his shirts and threw it on the bed. "It's way too big."

"So? Would u rather have something of vic-"

"No thank you." I quickly dried myself off with the towel and put the shirt on. "See perfect, you look adorable." He had grey sweats on and a tight white shirt. I gulped.

His hand wrapped around mine as a reflex I pulled away but I quickly grabbed his knowing it would get me in trouble. "What's going on with you." He says on the bed before grabbing the back of my thigh and pushing me tween his leg. His hands rubbed the back of my thighs.

Stop it Evelyn.

"Tell me. That's not a question Evelyn." He said sternly. His piercing and his dark eyes making him a lot more intimidating. "I just sometimes but I don't sometimes I just i feel weird" I looked away. "What does that mean?" His face looked weird, best described as — confused.

"Sometimes I feel like.." come on spit it out otherwise he will make u say it, he already is but ugh. I tried convincing myself. "Sometimes I feel sparks?" I didn't look at him. But I could see that stupid smile. The one he has when he's humiliating me.

"That's good to know." He smirked. I hated myself for the heartbeat between my legs. I shouldn't feel this way at all. "It's okay darling, no need to be ashamed? You're ours after all." He kissed my neck sending a wave of tension down my stomach. A unbelievable uncomfortable pain.

"Are you okay?" I nod trying to distract him. A smirk appeared on his face. Like he knew something he wasn't supposed to know. "Does ur stomach hurt?" My eyes widened. How would he know?

"It does."

I need a better poker face.

His face seemed scared. As if I had said something really bad. Is something wrong with me? "We have to check up right away." He sat me down on his lap. I gulped being so close to him yet him still being so much bigger then me. It scared me. Yet gave me a unnamable pleasure I couldn't describe.

"What's wrong?" I asked worried he spread my legs making my eyes widen. "I have to check if you're okay darling." He looked as if he wanted permission.

"Maybe something bad is happening? Or I can help the pain disappear." I nod. His finger moved along my slit down to my hole I looked down still too shy to look him in the eye when he touched me. Its not like I ever wanted it before.

Do I now?

No because he's checking.

His finger moved how he moved his hips. I bit my lip feeling ashamed at the pleasure I got from him checking up on me. "It's okay darling let it out its part of the process." I nod his thumb circled my clit causing a moan to slip out. His other hand on my back to keep me from falling over.

"Hmm, I think I have to add another finger to make sure I'm doing everything right." I nod letting him. He added another finger making my eyes squint in a painful way. Even tho they've fucked me. It doesn't really seem to affect the pain it causes every first time it goes in...

My entire body relaxed feeling a unimaginable pleasure wash over me. "Aw there we go." He held my back. My head resting on his shoulder as he slowly moved his fingers. "Does ur stomach feel better?" I nod. "Thank you.." I whispered. I dont think he was checking was he.. I felt myself doze off.

Second person

Elijah laid her under the covers making sure she was fully covered after she dozed off. Dropping to his knees next to the bed he laid his arms next to her sleeping, resting his chin on his arms he whispered "you really are something else, it sounds crazy, maybe because I've never had it before. But I really think you're the one. You're perfect for me. For us. No matter where you go I'll find you, I promise princess." He kissed her forehead making sure to seal the promise.

He closed the door behind him making sure to tell his brothers the amazing new tactic he had found to manipulate their little doll with. And the news he had heard from her lips himself.

~

Evelyn. I opened my eyes feeling sick. As soon as I woke up I noticed I wasn't in the room I fell asleep in, my eyes widened seeing a males back outside of the glass door.

I quickly grabbed what looked like a trash can and threw up.

Where am i?

I looked around feeling the ground move. Am i high? I fell to the wall and the person at the door turned around seeing me fall his face turned in shock hurrying into the room and helping me up.

"Are you okay miss?" He asked. I furrowed my brows my sight blurry. "You don't look very good." His face seemed to grow even more worried.

My hands grabbed his face trying to see it correctly. My eyes keep going in and out of blurriness. "Call the boss" he shouted to someone else in the hall.

"Did you hit your head?" He tried to look on my head for any injuries. Before he could move Elias walked into the room ripping him off. My eyes widened dropping my hands.

"Baby?" Theo came. "Why are you awake already? You're not supposed to be awake for another 6 hours." His eyes shifted to Elijah who now also saw I was awake.

"Why is she awake?" His gaze shifted to Elias and i began getting dizzy again. "Bucket" I pointed at the bucket. He quickly grabbed it and I threw up as he got it just in time.

Elijah pinched the bridge of his nose. Elias's face seemed like he was in pain. And Theo was still confused.

"She's sea sick." Elias said, Elijah exhaled loudly. "I told you to figure that out Theo, stupid fuck." He walked over to me shoving Theo away. My eyes blinked a lot more trying to keep them from going blurry. "You're going to be okay baby." I couldn't help but smile. "She's high." He looked up at Theo standing next to us with his hands in his pocket.

"Do you think you need to throw up any more?" I shook my head. I think I puked everything out. "Where are we?" Realisation set in.

"We are on a boat, well in." That doesn't help. "Where are we going?" Elias cleared his throat. "We're going to have to start telling her shit eventually." Theo spoke up. What? Telling me?

"He is right." Elijah looked at me then at Elias who shook his head. "She will hate u even more." Elijah looked at me again. I blinked my vision getting blurry everything sounded like we were underwater. Or like I was dreaming.

"We shouldn't speak ab this where she is anyways." Elias spoke. "We are going to our house, which is located in a secret location that we will tell you about when we get there." Elijah placed his hand on my cheek caressing it with his thumb. For some reason. It felt nice. It kills me to admit that.

How am I going to get away if we are somewhere i dont even know where we are.

I looked down thinking.

"What?" Theo came closer. My eyes widened. "What did u say?" I gulped backing away from him and Elijah who seemed to have the same face he had when he spoke to Victoria first...

"You still want to leave? Haven't you fucking learned you aren't going any fucking where Evelyn." My heart beat. Elijah did some sort of gesture and Elias took Theo out the room. The door closed but no guard returned.

Elijah looked down before kicking his shoes off and his belt. He crawled under the sheets while i remained inches away on-top of them.

He didn't force me under the sheets instead he began talking.

"You know, I understand why you want to leave." He put his arms under his head looking at me. I looked down holding my knees with my head ontop of them slightly looking at him in the corner of my eyes. "I do. I'm sorry we had to meet in these circumstances, I am. But I'm not sorry I met you. I don't care how long it takes for you to fall in love. I know you feel something. I know it. There's no way u dont. I mean, a lot of woman have tried to be in your place but you, you're the only one who's ever caught my attention. No I don't kill them. But I don't have interest in them so I just let them go and that's the end of it. With you. I never wanna let you go. And I won't."

He paused.

Inhaling before exhaling and looking at the ceiling. "If you do try leave, I'll find you." He quickly looked at me I looked forward avoiding eye contact. "You'll love me Evelyn. Youll love us. The way we love you. Because we do." I furrowed my brows looking at him.

"What?" He sat up his hair messy from laying on the pillow, his tongue piercing showed. He must be right. A lot of woman must've wanted to be in this place.

Maybe under different circumstances I would too.

"You don't love me." I looked away. He seemed offended. His hand grabbed my chin making me look at him.

His nose touching the tip of mine. My eyes widened. His breath touched my lips as he spoke. "Dont ever fucking say that again, Evelyn. I'm fucking serious." He threatened. The rasp in his voice made me look away.

"You'll love me too, I promise."

He kissed me. He wrapped his arms around mine as he laid me on-top of him unable to move my arms I sighed laying my on his chest. "Good toy."

Promises

E velyn.

I opened my eyes crunching my face as I felt something between my legs. "Oh goodmorning baby." His breath hit my neck I couldn't move my arms as he held my wrists down.

"I'm sorry baby I just couldn't resist it. I felt so frustrated all night, you don't mind right?" He kissed my neck. I felt ashamed for the way I felt butterflies.

This isn't normal ...

"That's right, I knew you didn't." He kissed my jaw all the way up to my face. "Elias" I felt my back arch as he kept hitting the same spot. "I know I know, you already came once darling I bet you don't remember." He bit my shoulder creating a bite mark. I gulped as I felt myself come.

"You like it rough dont u." His nails digged into my waist causing me to moan. I moved my face to the side shutting my eyes. "Getting so wet all over my dick bunny." I whined at him humiliating me.

"Stop." I managed to get through broken moans. "Stop what?" He hit the spot again harshly causing me to shiver. "It's so cute, you're such a little virgin." He smiled against my cheek before kissing it. I kept my eyes shut. Tried my best to hide my moan but he wouldn't let me.

"Come on dont you want me to hear? After all im making you feel better then anyone ever has. Oh that's right no one has. Ur all mine. Every inch of ur skin is mine." He bit my collar bone speeding up his thrusts.

"Feel that baby." He let go of my hand grabbing it and putting it on my stomach.

"You feel that?" I nod. "Tell me what is it?" He whispered in my ear taunting me. "It's your dick.." he kissed my cheek. "Well done dear." He grabbed my hips arching my back.

"You're just such a tiny little fuck doll I love fucking you. You're never leaving me." He repeated to himself. "Fucking tell me." My heart beat faster.

I couldn't help but hate myself even more for the weird pleasure in my upper stomach. The excitement.

"I'm never leaving you..." I whispered throughout sobs from over-stimulation. "That's right. Why would you? I treat you so good. I love you. You wont leave me? No. You wouldn't. Because you're mine. You're ours." He grabbed my face making me look at him his hands almost covering my entire head.

He seemed infatuated. Crazy. "Tell me." His thrusts didn't slow down. Instead they got harder. "I won't leave you because I'm yours"

I whispered he smiled. More like a grin. A crazy one. But for some sickening reason it turned me on.

"Such a well behaved toy. I love u." He kissed me before also releasing.

"No wait what if I get pregnant-" his hand covered my mouth. He moaned in my ear making me forget that.

~

After Elias Insisted on taking a shower together. I walked in the room to see a white little dress on the bed with sandals. White underwear next to it and a brush even tho I already had a brush.

I didn't remember getting to the house to whatever it is where we are now.

I quickly put on the clothes and brushed my long hair that had knits everywhere because of how rough they are.

I opened the door slipping my head out I jumped at Elijah smoking next to the door. I stepped out the room looking at him. "Trying to escape?" He put his hand out for me to take it. I did.

"No." I looked down. We walked down a long hall and at the end there were big white doors that led to a bigger entrée.

A big door on the left which seemed like the front door. There were pillars everywhere. My eyes widened.

"What?" He looked down as he ashes his cigarette in the plant. I furrowed my brows. "Hey!" I grabbed the cigarette out. "Throw it in the bin." I stood in-front of him looking up at him holding the scrunched up a-shed out cigarette.

He chuckled looking around making his Adam's apple clear, before looking back at me. "You're ordering me?" He went through his knees down to my level his face now infront of mine even tho he's basically sitting on his knees.

"I have maids, they'll clean it." He took it out of my hand and threw it behind him on the floor an amused grin on his face when I stomped on the ground annoyed. I went to go behind him but he dragged my arm back making me stumble.

"I said they'll clean it. You're not a maid baby." He picked me up. "I do like the dress on you, Theo picked it." I rolled my eyes. He put me down in a room with a big table. On his lap of course it's not like I can have any personal space ever.

"Goodmorning dolly." Theo put down his phone and Elias came in after kissing my cheek before sitting down.

"How did u sleep, after the sickness." Plates lowered onto the table by a short brunette woman. She didn't look at any of us before heading out again with a little bow. I watched her leave.

"I asked you something." I flinched looking back at Theo. "I'm sorry, I slept fine." I smiled. I need them to see I'm not going to leave so I can try...

"I slept good too thank u for asking." He cut into his pancakes I gulped. Elijah moved my hair to my back. Placing a kiss on my shoulder. "It's okay, he's a little agitated from work. Go sit with him hm?" It wasnt a question.

I nod getting up and walking towards Theo who already moved his chair back as soon as I stood up. I slowly walked trying to stall time but his hands wrapped around my waist pulling me towards him.

I looked down. "Here eat." He cut some pancakes up and fed them to me. I ate them as I hadn't ate anything for a while. And they're draining me in every possible way.

"So ur talking with that one guy who fucked up couple days ago right?" Elijah spoke to Elias who nod as he stated at me. I gulped feeling uncomfortable.

"Open." Theo fed me again. "And you're going to speak to that lady right?" Elijah moved to theo who made a "Hm" sound Elijah shook his head before taking out a little book. "You're going with me." He spoke to me.

"Where?" I don't want to go anywhere I don't wanna be here either. "Just dinner, nothing serious I have to discuss some things." I nod.

~

I slipped on the light green flower dress someone left on the bedroom I was returned to after Elijah made me sit with him through all his paper work. They're not letting me do anything alone.

No. Not right now either.

I smiled at Elijah who sat in the chair across from me near the windows. "Do you mind.." I sat pointing at the bathroom. He tilted his head in confusion. "Uh if I dress there..." his lips formed a little line before nodding. I whispered a small "Thank u.." before disappearing into the bathroom.

Okay Evelyn. This is the time to leave? There will be people there there's no way he can do anything? They'll help?

I smiled and nod frantically trying to calm myself down.

I exhaled loudly looking in the mirror.

These shoes make me a lot taller ... I smiled. I like it.

I walked out the bathroom. Elijah stood up too smiling his eyes seemed to be filled with a unrecognisable gloss. Almost desire.

"Come here." He moved his hand gesturing to come to him. I walked over to him. He turned my around taking the first two trains under my front strands and tying them to the back with a light green bow.

"Where did u learn how to do hair." I turned around catching myself genuinely smiling.

If you look at him. His stern face. Strong jaw line. Piercing. Dark eyes. He's a very dominating person in general. Even without all that once he stepped into the house a certain almost different air hit. Its suffocating in a way and calming i cant describe it. U want to leave it but u cant.

"Did u forget about Victoria." He smiled a little. "Oh yes of course." I looked down remember vic. She left me.. "are u okay?" His hand slipped around my lower back pulling me to him. I nod smiling. "Is it time to go?" He nod.

In the car it was silent for a bit. I already knew his had a gun with him. He wouldn't shoot me infront of people ri-

My thoughts were cut off by his voice.

"Oh also, don't make a scene Evelyn. This is my restaurant." My eyes widened. "You have a restaurant?" He nod.

Maybe it's because I don't come from Money but this is insane.

"Those people, they listen to me. Do not think you can escape there Evelyn it's even more guarded then my house.

I slightly gasped inside. I must've counted over 50 guards the two halls we walked ...

"Do you understand?" I nod. "I won't try anything.."

I gulped. Fuck.

~

Dinner had been going well. They were talking about, actually I have no idea they don't have to speak secretly because I don't know what all these words mean.

In this dinner I also learned Elijah can speak French Spanish and a bit polish which really surprised me. He said he had to learn during his training where all his scars come from too.

Elijah's hand hasn't left my thigh the entire night.

I jumped being brought back to the conversation went a girl stormed in the room. "Daddy he's being mean to me." She stomped her feet on the ground next to the male. I looked at Elijah who smiled at my and moved my chair more to him.

Not to calm me down.

Out of possession.

"He's being so mean he won't let me have a sprinkly ice cream because they don't have that and he won't get me one!" She balled her fists up in balls. "Baby, I'm in a meeting, I'll get you as many ice creams as u want when we go home okay?" He told her. She whined loudly in disapproval. The male who came in behind her supposedly being mean to her threw his hands up.

The male at the table pinched the bridge of his nose. "Baby, I can't deal with this now do you see." He pointed at me and Elijah. "I'm in a meeting you need to stop being a spoiled little brat for five minutes." He caressed her cheek and as if it wasn't bad enough.

She seemed really set off now. And a grin appeared on her face.

I smiled back trying to be polite.

"I want that one daddy!" She grinned widely putting her hands together and pouting her lips. "What?" He didn't understand. "I want her!" She pointed at me while jumping up and down tapping her feet around. Elijah chuckled.

"Uh, I'm afraid that's not going to happen baby see she already has someone." He explained. My brows furrowed. Am I for sale???

"I don't care I want her now!" She began sobbing. My lips parted. I've never seen anything like this.

And he can't be her dad... she doesn't look like a kid in her face apart for her expressions.

"Baby-" she began shouting no. "Take her out I'll be there in a couple mins we're almost done." She kicked and shouted but the male picked her up and walked her out.

"I hope you realise that she's not for sale." Elijah began before the guy could open his mouth. "I do realise that." He spoke in a byt form and opened his mouth again.

"I don't care about your offer. She's not for sale." His arm moved around my waist pulling me closer. "I understand." They began talking about their other thing again and i sat confused for the last 10 minutes.

"It was a pleasure speaking to you Mister Everest. And Mis Everest." He smiled shook Elijah's hand and walked out leaving me and Elijah alone.

"What just happened" I stared at the table in confusion.

"She's a little." He chuckled. "And quite a brat. You should know ur not getting away with that behaviour especially not in-front of anyone else she embarrassed the fuck out of him." He chuckled putting a cig in his mouth and lighting it.

"You shouldn't smoke." I mumbled he grabbed my waist putting me on his lap and he blew smoke out his nose. His eyes moved down to my dress, inhaling another puff of smoke.

"Why? Do you care if I die ten years earlier?" He chuckled throwing his head back over the end of the chair showing his Adam's apple perfectly. "It's not good for you." I looked away. He blew the smoke in my face making me cough. "You didn't answer my question. That tells me ur scared of answering it." He smirked.

"I guess that promise won't take that long will it Angel?" He smiled the smoke slowly leaving his mouth. The cig in his hand.

I bit my lip.

I couldn't resist it, I kissed him.

normal?

Evelyn.

I sat on the bed with a grin. "What?" He placed the pizza box on the bed. They all had their own pizza.

They can act like normal people and for some reason that makes me really happy.

"Nothing." I opened my pizza box taking a slice out and eating it. They are theirs too.

They don't normally act like normal people. So its hard for me to realise they are.

"So, at my conversation today, you remember D?" They nod. "His little wanted to buy ev" Theo laughed and Elias seemed annoyed.

"He tried but he knew it wasn't going to happen." He proudly ate another piece of pizza. "Yeah good, I'll kill her myself." Elias ate his food.

My brows scrunched.

Ew why would he talk about that while we eat.

"You're cute." Theo spoke to me. I shook my head looking at my already half eaten pizza.

I looked back at them who wouldn't stop staring at me. "What?" I looked at them putting my pizza down.

"Nothing, eat." Elijah demanded. I began eating. "You are acting weird." I looked a Theo's now annoyed face.

"No."

The next they wouldn't answer.

~

I put the box down next to the door. "Can I take a shower." They shared a look. "I'll check first." Elias got up and walked into the bathroom connected to the bedroom. "Eh, someone's gonna have to be in there with you." I shook my head.

"Oh i was coming anyways." Theo chuckled pushing my back towards the door of the bathroom.

Fuck.

He unzipped the back of my dress. Took the bow out. And slipped my underwear off.

"Perfect." He kissed my cheek quickly undressing himself he turned the shower on. I stood under it.

Of course it wasn't a normal shower it was a shower with glass doors. Two shower heads that were square above us streaming hot water down that already fogged the window up. A place you could sit in the wall like a little bench?

I looked up at his amused face he grabbed shampoo putting it in my hair.

He did everything for me shaving me everywhere. Washing my hair. All the way down to fucking me in the steaming hot shower.

And he definitely made sure his brothers knew.

And they made sure that I knew they knew by the smirk on their faces.

My legs were still sore from the 3 orgasms he forced me to have. He sat me down on Elias' slap who took the towel Theo handed him and softly started drying my hair.

A lot less hard then the others did. I shivered pulling the towel over my shoulders it still fully covered me thank god.

He stopped drying my hair and slowly moved my towel to the side showing my hard nipple from the cold. I looked away embarrassed. He smiled pinching it.

I yelped moving off his lap but his hands pulled me back. His thumb moved over the scar, his name right below my breast. "I'll always be with you." He kissed it making Me shiver.

"You drive me insane you know." His hands sat on my waist. My eyes widened the cold steel from his rings on my skin. I looked down feeing his bulge. "Your fault." His finger pressed onto my scar making me bite my lip. "Do you think u can take care of it baby?" I furrowed my brows whining.

"U only have to use ur pretty mouth." He grabbed my chin his thumb on my lip. I opened my mouth not wanting to anger him. He grabbed the tip of my tongue making me stick it out. I looked up at him his thumb rubbed over my tongue.

"Just perfect." He grabbed below my arms lowering me onto the ground. Before he took off his sweats he gestured Elijah to give him something.

A camera?

I looked at him. "What? You're mine I can film you whenever I want." He kissed my forehead. I gulped. He took his sweats off his bulge sprung free my eyes widened.

Second person

Evelyn looked up her eyes filled with fear, but that only turned Elias on more. Clicking the button on the right he turned the film on.

He has a thing for pictures, specifically Polaroids. And old movie videos. The same as this one is filmed on.

He once again grabbed her chin his thumb gesturing her tongue open. She inched forward taking the tip into her mouth. "There we go ."

"Wrap your hands around the rest sweetheart" Elijah commented. She nod wrapping her hands around it.

She swirled her tongue around the tip causing Elias to chuckle. "Baby hey," he grabbed a hand full of her hair. "Who taught u that." He seemed surprised.

"Did I do something wrong?" She could feel fears prickle at her eyes a rock in her throat. "No no." He seemed in shock from the immense pleasure she gave him.

Is it because I'm in love with her?

He continued to let her to it herself and was pleasantly surprised at how well she did "Good girl, baby, go on." He moaned throwing his head back.

She closed her eyes embarrassed from how wet all of this was making her.

She kept trying to remind herself she had to leave. But the will to actually escape got smaller each day.

"Okay, baby stop stop." He says up but she didn't. Sucking and swirling her tongue he came down her throat. "Baby-" he couldn't help his moans spilling out. The groans. Curses. They drove her insane. She licked the tip clean.

"You really think I'll let you go anywhere after that?" He grabbed ahold of her throat lifting her up to her feet and kissing her.

"All fucking mine." He bit her lip a tear rolled down her cheek. He licked the blood off her lip and her the tear off her cheek.

He was once again infatuated.

She shook scared in his crazy grinning expression. He pulled his sweats up and held her, literally holding her hands over her and not letting her go. "You cant ever leave." He kissed her shoulder.

Evelyn.

"I cant have u leave do u understand?" I nod "I cant Evelyn."

"I won't.." I gulped feeling the same rock in my throat.

"Good, because I will lock u up unlike Elijah , I promise."

As if I am not already there 50+ guards in the hall and im not allowed to shower on my own.

I nod.

"Good." He smiled. "You need sleep."

I looked down nodding and he carried me over to the bed where Elijah was already laying. They put a movie on and help me. My legs and feet on Elijah, my waist on Theo. And my heat on Elias's lap.

He caressed my hair causing my eyes to shut.

"i love you." he kissed my head.

"iloveutoo." i whispered dozing off.

second pov

Elias smiled at how fast she replied. There was no disobedience, no resisting.

"I think shes starting to get used to us." Theo spoke up and Elias nod. "Its because the more shes around us the softer we become." Elijah spoke up and Theo grinned.

"we havent ate pizza on a bed like that since we were what 13 years old? that one time we got high out of our minds and laughed the entire night because Theo fell asleep with a slice on his face." they thought back to something that wouldve seemed so silly now but it was a precious memory.

a memory she brought back.

Elijahs hand caresses her legs feeling thankful. even tho he doesn't exactly know how to show it.

misunderstanding

E velyn.

I opened my eyes slightly whimpering from still feeling sore.

To my surprise no one was there. No one in the room. I slowly got up the covers slipping off me.

I have no clothes..

I quickly looked around. The bathroom? I opened the door. No one... I looked at the clothes on the ground. I groaned picking up Theo's big shorts and a shirt. I quickly put them on tying a not in the back of the shorts so they wouldn't fall off.

I walked over to the door opening it i was surprised as it unlocked and there were no guards by the hall.

I softly walked to the big white doors that led to the main part of the house. I opened the door walking out.

My eyes widened when I saw them standing beside the door.

There were two men standing before every door. There are 6 like a octopus of halls leading to other rooms I assume.

"What is she doing out?" They didn't bother asking me anything. "Uh i was looking for Elijah or uh theo-" he grabbed my upper arm firmly making me crunch my face up in uncomfort.

"where are we going" I asked the didn't answer we walked quicker then I could keep up but eventually there was a big white door with another two guards next to it. "Boss is almost done." He answer, the guard holding me nod walking off with me again.

I gulped. Where are we going now...

My eyes widened at what seemed like a office. Three desks.

Can they not do anything alone?

I tried to get my arm out of his hard grip. "Can u let me go" He looked at me. I could feel the frustration in his eyes. I gulped. His hand raised i closed my eyes there was nothing else I could do.

He's almost 7' tall and he won't let me go.

As if on cue the door opened and Elijah walked in with Theo and Elias behind him who were joking around.

Second person.

"What a dumb asshole." He laughed holding his hand over his lower chest. "You love making fun of people." Elias rolled his eyes but joked with him.

Elijah was busy with his phone to have the next meeting ready. Since it was almost 11:30 am he could head by the office before Evelyn woke up. Or so he thought.

The doors opened and Elijah looked up seeing a figure in the room.

Theo already had his gun out. "What the fuck are you doing." Elijah stepped closer pulling Evelyn out of the man's grip. Elias's eyes already went blank of any emotion.

Evelyn's eyes were full of tears. The guns. The intensity. She was scared to death. And you could tell with the way she shook in Elijahs embrace.

"She tried to escape." He said. Evelyn's jaw dropped tears spilled as she choked on her sobs. "That's not true! I was looking for you I asked him!" She looked up at Elijah who had a questioning look on his face. But he wouldn't question her infront of anyone.

He looked up at Theo who brought the other guard in. "What happened." He ordered. The man didn't know what was going on. He explained how Evelyn came walking in and asked for Elijah. Elijah's tongue poked his cheek showing he was really pissed off.

"So you touch something that's fucking mine and then you have the guts to lie to my face?" He chuckled sending a shiver down Evelyn's spine.

As if on cue all of them went blank Theo picked up Evelyn carrying her as Elijah grabbed the back of the man's neck and dragged him out to the main part of the house.

He threw the guard on the ground causing him to land on his knees, his loud deep voice rang through each halls as hundreds of guards serounded the room.

Elijah waved his hand and Theo handed Evelyn.

"Now listen up you fucking idiots." He got his gun out of the back of his belt and shot a hole through the guys head causing his body to collapse to the floor. Evelyn shook the blood splattered across her aswell.

She could feel her throat swell up.

"If any of you even look at her in a disrespectful way, you won't be off this easy. I'll hand you over to Elias and Theo. And I'll definitely deal with you myself too." He spoke sternly. "Do not fucking touch her." All of them nod and said yes boss as they went back to their own places.

Elias hurriedly walked over to the room they had been staying in with Evelyn as he noticed she was having a panick attack.

"Evelyn calm down baby." He tried to calm her down but it wasn't working. By this time Elijah and Theo also noticed they were gone and hurried to the room.

They quickly sat down where they sat on the floor since she collapsed when they walked in. "Evelyn breathe." Elijah ordered but she couldn't.

Evelyn sat in Elijah's lap as he whispered sweet nothings into her ear how it's okay. "Hey hey, baby it's okay I'll never hurt you?" He caressed here hair as he noticed it calmed her down before.

"You killed him." She shook her eyes full of tears. "He left a hand print on your arm angel, he hurt you." She looked up at him not knowing how to feel. "It's okay, he was on thin ice anyways it's not your fault okay?" Elijah moved.

After a while she was okay and he wiped her tears away kissing her cheeks until she giggled.

"So why were you looking for me?"

Evelyn.

I could feel his tongue piercing against my tongue as he kissed me before pulling away. "Why were you looking for me?"

"Uh well there was no one here and i was wondering where you were." I looked at him who looked at their and Elias.

"Darling." He began i nod. "You'll be staying with Elias today okay?" I nod. "But where are you going?" He smiled and kissed my cheek while stroking my hair. "Just doing some work, you'll stay with Elias so your not alone." He set me down on the bed.

"Your going already?" He bend down to my level and caressed my cheek. "I have things to do soon I'll be done okay? Im trying to get everything finished so we can spend as much time with you as possible darling." He kissed my forehead while grabbing his jacket and walking out.

Theo kissed me, "you better behave dolly remember, Elias can be a lot harsher then he looks." He kissed my cheek before also walking out.

I looked at Elias who looked beyond excited.

"so what do you want to do my pretty baby?" he spoke up. I shrug sitting on the bed. "i got you some clothes." he smiled. "and if you behave you can have your own room." my own room?

theyre starting to trust me. why do i feel bad for still trying to escape?

"thank you." i smiled. "Evelyn?" he spoke up walking towards me. "yes?" i replied he sat down on the bed next to me.

"have u ever smoked?" he asked i shook my head. i know that he smokes and Elijah does i dont know about theo tho.

"Would u want to try?" I shook my head. "I don't see a point in smoking cigarettes." He chuckled. "Not cigarettes, weed." I furrowed my brows.

"I mean I have always wanted to try..". He smirked walking out. I could hear a click meaning he locked the door.

I quickly went over to the pile clothes that laid on the desk. The room was very simple. A bed. Bathroom. A desk and just some other basic stuff. It kind of looks like when you go to home shops and they have the rooms ready for u to pick out of.

There's no personal stuff. No letters in any drawers. The windows have locks. So do the doors. Other then that the room is a white with light blue colour.

I slightly jumped as the door unlocked again and Elias came in with a glass thing. I looked at him confused as he put down a little box as well.

"What is this.." I looked at the long glass thing. It was rounder at the bottom with a long uh stick?

"It's called a bong." I looked up at him puzzled. "But I've only ever seen people smoke them as cigarettes?" He took out a little pot with green things in it.

Another round thing with spikes inside.

"You seem very confused baby." He chuckled. "I love how your brain is so innocent you get so fascinated by everything.

Elias.

I watched as she observed me stuffing the bong with the green buds. I wont let her hit this right away because she wont come down from it but she can smoke and maybe eat an edible. Or I just let her pick.

I took out the little bag I had peach rings in. Her eyes went big and glossy. Sometimes I just take in how beautiful she is. Like how she looks at me right now.

That curious look in her eyes is exactly what makes me wanna carve pretty messages in her. Everyone will see she's mine. Well ours.

I put the bong on the Floor and held the bowl in my hands. Without my knowledge she had already ate 3 out of 5 peach rings. "Uh Evelyn-" my eyes went big.

Oh shit.

Those were meant for me She could have one but it's on my weight and shit on what I can handle. She's having 3.... I took it out her hands and she swallowed the last. "Those are so yummy." She smiled. "I'm glad u think so angel" I'm so luckily I have a good poker face. She cant freak out.

"So should I try that?" She said pointing at the joint. I smiled. She so eagered to learn stuff. Its cute. I nod. Lighting the joint in my mouth I blew smoke into hers before handing off the joint to her.

She looked at me with big glossy eyes. She looks so fucking cute.

She took a hit inhaling it and coughing it out. I went to the bathroom to grab a glass of water. "Uh Evelyn-" I quickly walked over grabbing the candy. "But i like theseeee" she said holding onto my arm. "Baby u cant have any more." I said now only seeing one left.

She's gonna be high for the whole day and it's only ... 12.30... shit. Fuck.

I smiled caressing her hair. "Come on sit down!" She said.

Its cute when she's like this. I like it when she pays interest to us gives us the attention we deserve from her and only her.

"Okay baby, you wanna try again?" she nod taking the joint out of the ashtray and lighting it. She looks hot lighting it, fuck. Help.

Okay get urself together.

Safe place.

E lijah.

I pressed my lips into a line hearing my people speak on what's been happening in the industry. My brows raised hearing something. Disgust laced my face and they all knew it. I could see Ezra shake in fear. I crossed my arms turning to Theo who also had the same expression.

"How many fucking times do I need to tell you people we do not involve kids?" I clenched my jaw trying to get it out without ripping their heads off.

Especially with what happened with us as kids. There's no way I want any kid to go through that.

"But its good for the business-" I cut him off with my hand in the air. "Ezra. This is your last warning. Louise, watch this asshole." I stood up straightening my blazer. "If i get called for something like this again, That will be your last call." I walked away annoyed.

we can go home to evelyn now.

"you know Evelyn still doesnt know what we do right." i nod. "she asked me, i told her to look up our last name" my eyes widened. "are you stupid? she will want to get away even more." i sighed already annoyed I really need to see hee. we both walked to the car.

"the sooner she knows the sooner she can get used to it. she will know someday lijah." i clenched my jaw. she doesnt have to know. ever.

"its bes-" i cut him off. "will you fuck off, she doesn't need to know yet, and stop calling me that."

"whatever u want shes gonna figure it out shes not stupid, the guns, gaurds, etc." maybe im being stubborn, naive. i dont care. i dont want her to know now. maybe later. very far in the future.

second person.

Evelyn laid on the soft bed as she could feel her entire world fall away. All her worries. Every thought she had. Including the ones of escaping. Gone.

All she saw was Elias in the most prettiest form she had ever seen him.

Her small hands laid on his cheeks. Barely covering them.

"You're so pretty." It was like she had never seen his deep dark eyes. The way they made her feel like she was melting away. She couldn't tell if it was because of the weed or because of him. After all she didn't know how weed felt.

"Why does this feel so.." she tried to find the words but she couldn't. It didn't help that she ate 4 weed gummys for a grown man either.

Elijah and Theo walked in as they saw what had happened they quickly understood the advantage they had. Elijah threw his blazer off, together with his shoes. "I need a shower." Theo went into the bathroom leaving Evelyn with Elias and Elijah. All their frustration, annoyance. Gone. At the sight of their baby laying so helplessly.

Elijah bend down but before he could kiss Evelyn she returned the kiss opening her mouth. His hand held the back of her head deepening the kiss. She moaned feeling his tongue piercing.

"Needy arent we?" Elijah chuckled at Evelyn's state. She whined not really knowing why she suddenly felt so attracted to them. She looked up at him with big eyes causing his lips to crash back onto hers. "You know i cant resist u when u look at me like that." He kissed down her jaw softly whispering.

Elias couldn't wait to carve Elijah and Theo's name into her aswell grabbing his special knife he made sure to find a perfect spot on the waist. Too distracted by Elijah and the high she had she couldn't feel anything but the euphoria coming from the cut.

She bit Elijah's lip causing him to smirk, at that moment Theo also came out. And he picked her thigh to put his name on. Elias made sure to deeply carve im all of their names written out fully.

Elias. Elijah. Theodore.

He was happy about it. It gave him the satisfaction that she would never leave. Not that they would ever let her. She was their perfect play thing. The perfect doll to play with.

Ofc they loved it even more when she enjoyed it aswell.

In their eyes they weren't possessive. Nor obsessive. You should love someone to ur fullest ability. And they did. They had made her her own room. Trying to give her more trust. And after this they were sure she could have it.

They wanted her to feel more free. But not too free. She must not forget she cant leave after all?

Elias watched as her lips parted. Elijah softly sucked on her nipple and Theo lazily tried off his hair enjoying the view. A gorgeous empty canvas for me to destroy.

Elias couldn't control his thoughts. It was hard for him to share at moments. especially when it came to her. But he managed. Especially with the way she laid down beautifully on the pillow. Her eyes shut. Lips slightly parted. Her cheeks had a slight pink gloss over them.

She softly bit her lip not letting any more whines out which caused Elias to press into her deeper. She moaned again. Sending a shiver down all of them. Unimaginable feelings none of them could describe.

But they all had it.

They all knew exactly what they felt but they couldn't describe it. It was her. She was the only one that had ever made them feel that way. They dated as teenagers and adults but never found the girl for them. They either claimed to be submissive but weren't at all.

And its not like they weren't up for a challenge, especially Theodore.

But its not what they wanted.

Evelyn is everything they've ever wanted.

Soft, but not too soft to handle stuff. Harsh in a sweet way.

She was perfect.

And they weren't planning on letting her go anytime soon. She just needed to realise the same thing.

She couldn't help but feel bad for enjoying everything but the high took that away. She knew she was attractive to them. Who wouldn't be. Their dark energy. Piercings. Tattoos. Their height. Built. Manners in the way they are supposed to have them. They confused her.

The way they treated her but could be so polite with her. How they were the upmost soft while trying to dress her. Or figure out how to braid her hair. They loved taking care of her and it confused her. Especially since she always only took care of herself.

But they way they hurt her also turned her on, and that was the most confusing thing for her.

Freedom.

E velyn.
   I opened my eyes. My head feels like it's spinning. Two arms harshly hugged me against them. By his finger tattoos I can tell it's Theo. I tried to move but I couldn't. I widely opened my eyes seeing I was in a new room.

"Baby please go to sleep." He sleepy groaned into my ear. "I'm not sleepy.." I whispered, he groaned. "Please?" I softly smiled, "can I turn?" He rested his arms letting me face him. My face heat up as I watched his face soft.

His lips so kissable. His eyes shut. They're so peaceful when they sleep. I softly moved some of his hair out of his face. I looked down as he chuckled. "It's okay to like us back you know." He smiled as i huffed. "I do not." He finally opened his pearly dark eyes. My eyes widened. "You have green eyes??"

My lips parted as he nod. His long eyelashes made his eyes look much darker from further. "Just like yours." He kissed my forehead.

"Yours are a lot prettier tho." He smirked not letting me go. "Where are we?"

He seemed taken aback. "Your room?" I shook my head, "uh i dont have a big room like this.." I looked down embarrassed. His face softened. "It's all yours, baby doll." He kissed my cheek.

"How did you know I like light green?" He smirked. "I cant give away all my secrets now can I?" I knit my brows. Softly slapping his chest. He dramatically gasped "look who's getting brave!" He chuckled still holding me in his arms. "Please tell me." I frowned making my eyes big.

He chuckled. "Hmm, that may work on Elias and Elijah but u got the wrong one dolly". He made sure to remind me of his sadistic self. He loved to taunt me. He really enjoys it. "How late is it?" He moved his wrist up looking on his watch. "It's 11:13 am." I suddenly remembered last night.

"Am I still high?...how did I get here? Did I fall asleep?" Theo's hand softly moved away my hair. "Darling, you took 4 weed gummies that weren't meant for your uh, well size. So it will probably still affect you a little but not much you'll be okay after a shower." He smiled. I nod. "Can I have a shower?"

He nod letting me out of his arms. "Alone?" He nod again and my eyes lit up. I haven't had a single alone shower yet I think. Elias said they were scared I would try kill myself...

I sat on the edge of the bed Theo sat up grabbing a cig but quickly putting it away as I dont smoke. "So I'm allowed to be alone?" Theo's face softened but his dark atmosphere never leaves him.

"We want to give u some space to figure out what, you want. Because we know we want you. Only you." He looked down as a child that couldn't fully get out of his words. My face softened as I watched him fidget with the blanket.

"We want You to actually like us back.." he mumbled a bit. "Maybe if you have space you can figure it out?" I could see him getting more nervous with every word he spoke out.

"Anyways you need a shower u stink." He kicked me off the bed causing me to gasp. "I do not stink!"

I knew it was because he couldn't get any more out. He felt too vulnerable and that's their issue. They cant be vulnerable.

I walked into the bathroom smiling as there were countless of shampoos shaving things scents bath bombs countless of pretty light green towels, tampons and pads in all shapes and sizes.

i walked out again. "you like it?" he seemed hesitant to ask. scared to ask. "I love it, who got it?" I asked. "Uh we tried our best.." he scratched his neck.

I couldn't help but smile. I quickly walked back into the bathroom. "You did a goodjob." I yelled closing the door and sliding down it.

What do I want?

I obviously find them attractive. But I need to get away right? Ugh.

I gripped onto my hair with both my hands. I didn't lock the door as I dont think they would really like that. I collected myself got up and turned on the beautiful shower.

The room was better then the one we were in before. It was similar built but still different. The bathroom was white with a dark almost woods green col. Its beautiful.

I cant wait for it to rain.

Maybe what I need is a conversation with them? A real one? I nod. I washed the soap out my hair. I furrowed my brows as I saw it was the exact same honey lavendel shampoo I use at home. Coincidence ?

I dried my hair off leaving it to air dry. Its getting really long. I smiled its the only thing that's ever made me feel really pretty. I walked out seeing them all in my room i quickly stopped the towel still around me.

"Goodmorning dear." Elijah smirked as he leaned against the little white desk. "Goodmorning." I softly smiled walking to my closet. "There." Elias pointed at the bed. Ofc he picked something out again.

I looked at the pink set of panties and the white cute dress. I smiled looking at it. "Dear?" Theo watched as I took in the room. The clothes. Everything.

A tear rolled down my cheek and I could feel Elijah hug me from behind his head on my shoulder. "Is it not good?" I shook my head softly. "It's perfect.." top perfect. I should be happy. I must come over so ungrateful... "thank u.." I whispered. I could see Theo's smile return. Along with a small one on elias's face.

"It's okay, you're safe." Elijah whispered against my neck. I nod. I grabbed the dress and the underwear letting my towel drop their eyes widened. "Uh..." I looked at them as if something was wrong.

"Nothing dear go on." Elijah adjusted himself. I furrowed my brows. I could see them share looks but I couldn't understand.

Second person.

Elijah had a busy life with his business, but he didn't love studying anything more then his precious little toy. He enjoyed seeing her eyes light up when he gave her something he knew she never had.

He knew she was grateful for it. Simply because of the little expressions in her face.

They went by her apartment to check on anything she may want to keep. They also bought the place for her and when the landlord said they weren't allowed they bought the whole building just incase she wanted to keep her apartment.

He let go of her and she dropped her towel making all their stomach flutter with butterflies they never felt. Something about her showing herself to them like that made them feel a lust they couldn't control.

A need they had to satisfy.

Elias wanted to rip the dress right off her again as she asked Theo to zip it up. Theo didn't mind showing his bulge since he knew how much she wanted to please them. He knew she didn't want to disappoint them. Or tho he thought so. And somewhere he was right.

She turned around seeing her eyes land on his bulge he smirked. She quickly looked away gulping when she noticed they were all frustrated. Elijahs lips pressed into a line he stood uncomfortably. And Elias was ready to walk out.

"Wait.." she softly spoke as Elias's hand grabbed onto the handle. "Maybe I can help..." she didn't know if she regretted her words, all she knew was that she was equally as needy.

Disrepect.

E lijah.

"Evelyn hurry up I Dont have all day." I said as she slowly undressed herself. "Why am i not allowed to shower alone?" Why would u want to spend time away from me?

"Why cant u listen? Hm." I took it upon myself to take her clothes off since it goes a lot quicker. Taking off my own I stepped into the shower as-well. Her tiny body between the wall and my body.

No where to go.

She knew not to protest by now.

It has no use. She flinched feeling my hands in her hair spreading the shampoo around. "Today we're going out." I announced.

She softly nod. I took the detachable shower head next to us on the wall and washing her hair out with it. "Are you going to be good?"

I pressed my body against her not getting an answer she was softly pressed against the wall. She held her hands up trying to not get squished.

I cant say she doesn't look adorable.

"Hm?" I bend down waiting for an answer my head on her shoulder as she nervously breathed onto the cold stone. "I will.."

"Do you remember how to announce us baby?" I kissed her shoulder. Her breathe hitched making me slightly smirk. She's adorable. Its hard to be harsh on her like this but she needs to understand, leaving isn't an option. Dying isn't either.

She is not going anywhere.

"What was that?" I mocked her pathetic whimper. "Yes daddy.." her forehead pressed against the stone probably to cool down. My hand wrapped around her neck pulling her body under mine right under the stream of the shower head.

"There we go." I picked her up her face facing me. I softly kissed her. Her legs wrapped around my waist and her back attached to the cold stone.

"Stop it, it wont hurt so much." I whispered softly fucking into her. "Please.." she whimpered her nails still scratching at my back. "No." I positioned my hands on her ass lifting her up.

She choked on her own spit making me laugh. Her cute little face turning all red from embarrassing followed by a whimper.

Adorable.

The way her tiny body trembles beneath me sends me even more over edge. I dont think I'll ever get enough of her. I don't ever want to.

"It hurts." She tried to convince herself. But even her body didnt. Beautiful moans followed not even half way through her words. "What did you say?" I softly bit her skin.

The steam from the shower fogging the entire shower up more, along with her mind.

I smiled when she finally broke and moaned loudly. "You're close aren't you?" Her vicious nods made me slow down my thrusts earning a whine.

Spending them up again I talked into her ear holding her body closely to mine. "Repeat everything I say and maybe I'll let you cum, cum before I finish what I want u to say and you'll be cuming a lot more ti ones then you want." Her lip trembled as I looked her straight in the eyes.

"I love being fucked by you like a dumb whore..." I smile as the horror of having to repeat those words herself grows bigger.

"I love being fucked like a dumb whore by you." cant even properly think stupid doll. Thats not what I said but I'll let it slide.

"i love being owned by you" i could tell she was getting closer each harsh thrust that slammed into her tiny body.

"I love being owned by you daddy." She quickly moaned out. I smiled at her need of pleasing me. "I won't try run away ever again." I wrapped my hand around her waist harshly thrusting her down onto me. "I won't try run away again" she choked out her eyes fluttering closed and open.

My other hand at the back of her head so it won't touch the cold stone and hurt her.

"Please." She begged repeatedly it frantically not being able to restrain any longer. "Go on doll." I watched as she fell apart, slowly began shaking and completely settled into me. I washed her off before carrying her to my room and setting her down. Her unconscious pretty face from being fucked too much is my favourite sight to see. She's had her own room for a couple days now. But I prefer having her close to me.

Due to our jealousy involving the night. We all take her whenever it's our night. I know I've had her yesterday but I deserve another night with her.

I picked out some clothes I had for her. A black long dress and black little heals. Its easy getting her dressed.

I like taking care of her. I picked up her right leg putting on her black matching panties and bra. We asked her if she likes to wear it, I don't think she knows we care. Maybe we don't show it enough.

If we do she might think we're soft, and leave.

I placed my hand under her neck sitting her up and sitting behind her as I put the bra on her as-well. She said it makes her uncomfy when she doesn't wear them and it hurt her collarbones when she doesn't.

She's mine. Ours. Forever.

I cant imagine a life without her and I won't have one without her. I softly placed her under my sheets.

Drying off I looked at the stitching above my v-line. Fucker.

I tried off throwing on some grey sweatpants and a white shirt. I know it somehow affects her. She says she doesn't like us but her body language says a different thing.

Especially compared to how scared other people are of us. She's not nearly as frightened.

I dont know if that's a good thing or a bad thing. She did try leave before. I hope she doesn't make us take harsher matters. I stroked her cheek as she softly slept.

At that moment my phone went. I sighed looking at my baby. I would truly leave everything behind for her. We have enough money resources we can go. But I need her to want that.

I stood up grabbed my phone off my desk.

Luscious ; the job is done.

One of my best men. He truly doesn't disappoint ive been thinking about assigning him to Evelyn. To watch out around her. But I don't know if I can do that to the thriving kill he has inside him. And on-top if that I think Evelyn would have a heart attack.

I need to find someone to be with her when I need to do my shit. I quickly put my phone down when I heard her softly groan and sit up.

I crossed my arms sitting against the desk I looked at my watch. 5:14 pm.

"Morning sunshine." She looked at me with big eyes. "This isn't my room.." I shook my head. "No, after your little act i dont think u deserve to be there right now do you?" I watch as she looks at me dumbfounded.

She shook her head. I smirked. "Words." Ive been too easy with her not speaking. She doesn't understand that isn't her choice to make. I decide if she speaks. "No daddy." Her cheeks coated a harsh pink from embarrassment. She makes it so hard not to rip her clothes apart every five fucking seconds.

Confusion.

- -

E lijah.

"That's not even actually playing he just fucking pressed every single button, fucking moron" I sighed as Theo complained about Elias playing a game with him in the middle of my time with Evelyn.

"Theodore." I looked at him then at my bed where Evelyn was holding her laugh. So much for not soft she's literally laughing at us.

His eyes widened a stupid smile spread across his face the one he always has when he does things wrong.

"Evelyn here." I deadpanned and her smile dropped. Her eyes slightly widened but she walked over because she knew it would end worse otherwise.

"Here's your dress." She looked at it a soft smile back on her lips that quickly faded when she looked up at me. For some odd reason it made a little stab swing through my heart. But i didn't allow her to see.

"Thank you, daddy." She took the dress. I put my hand out for her to take it and she did. Her soft small hand barely covered half mine. I carefully helped her stay steady as she stepped into her dress.

It fit beautifully it was a bit low to the ground but that was only because she wasn't wearing the heals it was supposed to be with. "Beautiful darling." Elias commented.

She looked at him giving him a small smile. "What did I say about using your words?" She looked at me her big glossy eyes begging me to not make her say it.

"That's not very polite?" I grabbed her jaw harshly bringing my face closer to hers she began panicking. "I'm sorry daddy I will be polite." She quickly rushed out causing me to smile.

There we go.

Wasn't that hard to break, just need to put some time into it. "Thank you sir." She looked at Elias.

I like making her say things because it makes her nervous, and it turns us on when she properly talks to us.

"U do look very pretty dolly." Theo said pure to make her say it to him too. I could see the smug on his face. "Thank you master.." she looked down.

"Aw thats not how it works bunny, you look at Elias and Elijah but you wont give me the satisfaction of seeing your pretty face when you tell me?"

She looked at me then Theo clear panic settled in her eyes as the teasing was overbearing her. I smiled watching her cheeks turn even more red. "Thank u master." she looked at him.

A small chuckle left his lips before he spoke again, "I think I deserve a sorry too, dont u bun?" She softly nod. "I'm sorry master".

~

"I'm not hungry.." she said looking into her lap. Theo sighed. "You haven't ate in a while tho u need to eat something." She looked at me before looking back at her plate. "But I don't feel hungry." She shrugged.

"Evelyn, come here."

Theodore.

We watched as Evelyn walked over and Elijah lifted her up onto his lap. He took some scrambled eggs onto his fork and placed it at Evelyn's lips. She softly shook her head. Not how she normally does.

I dont know what Elijah did but she's scared shitless.

His face hardened and i could see his hand tighten around her arm. "Let her go Elijah." I stood next to them he looked up at me with a disgusted look. More so as if he felt disrespected.

"Off, now." I said as if he was a dog taking Evelyn I carried her out of her room.

She had slight tears at the rim of her eyes and she was visibly shaking.

I walked into my wing letting her into my room she sat on my bed. I sat against the head of the bed with her between my legs. She sat facing me.

"Are you okay baby?" I asked her trying to sound as sympathetic as I can without letting the curiosity of why he's so aggressive peak through.

I let my hand rest over my leg if she wanted to grab it she can if not I won't force her to.

"Doll?" She looked up and nod. "Why is Elijah being harsh on u?" Her eyes widened a little at the question.

She must've done something she knows wont go past me or Elias either. And she knows better then to lie to me.

"I did something.." I gave her a moment to finish her sentence but she didn't. "What did u do?"

"i dont want to say." she began fidgeting with ger shirt. "darling, its best to tell me. Elijah is probably telling Elias right now, im the last chance you got." her eyes widened at the thought of Elias knowing.

she looked down at her thigh. my name. i smiled. "come on, be good it'll get u further?" She nod softly biting her lip.

"I opened my window..." my jaw clenched but I tried to hide it. When she got her own room she got rules. No opening the windows when we aren't there.

"And then I saw these gorgeous flowers. Like a little garden." She mumbled. "It's been a long time since I've stood in grass." She exhaled loudly. "But Elijah got blinded and thought I was trying to leave." She looked up at me.

I softly smiled at her. "I hope you're telling me the truth darling. For now I'll take it but if it isn't. It'll be a lot worse." I spread my arms she laid on my chest.

"We do have a place to attend dear, you don't have that dress on for nothing." She created space between us making me slightly huff.

"Where are we going?" She seemed excited. "We have to meet a client." She nod.

That moment Elias and Elijah came in and Elias had what we call his crazy eyes. It sounds funny but it really isn't. He didn't move. He just stared at Evelyn before storming off again.

A.n hi!! Uploads might be a bit slower as I'm getting back into studying irl, I hope u understand thank u for reading <33

Pills.

T heodore.

    I smiled as she put on the mask we got specifically made for her. "Why do I need to wear this?" She asked probably not used to it all. I know since I did some digging into her past to figure out who she really is.

"We're going to a Masquerade ball darling." I tried to make her more excited but she didn't really know what it was from what I could tell.

"Where's Elijah? And Elias? Are they still upset.." she looked down as I tied the two strands of hair behind her head.

"I don't think they're upset Evelyn." I sighed grabbing her waist and putting her on one side of my thigh still facing me. Her legs dangled over the floor as she sat side ways.

"Remember when I told u to just look our name up?" She nod. "Elijah hates that, Elijah wants to somehow have u listen without scaring u." I escaped rubbing up and down her waist.

"But I will listen?" she said looking up at me with big glossy eyes almost pleading. "You will?" She nod.

I smiled. "Okay then." Ill give her a challenge then. If she really thinks she listens that well. "Here open" I instructed her.

I smirked when she actually opened her mouth and allowed me to enter her mouth with my tongue handing over the little pink pill. She had no idea I had it here.

She swallowed it without asking. "Good." I stood up walking towards the door. "Where are you going?" She asked standing behind me.

Its hard not to become softer with her around.

I held my hand out and she happily took it.

I think we should be a lot easier on her. Even tho it bugs me that she even wanted to go out and touch the grass i can understand it and my brothers should too.

Especially with the way we were raised.

The guards don't look up at her anymore because I told them if they do I'll stab their eyes out.

"I've never been in your room.." was the first thing she said as she entered. I smiled.

"It's very much like you.." she said sitting on the bed. The dress looked gorgeous, especially on her.

She doesn't know but we spend a very long time looking and designing this specifically fit for her. So no one else will ever be able to have the same one as her.

I put on my suit, a black blouse and some black pants, my black blazer. I know Elijah rather has me wear white, but he wears black with a red blouse only Elias actually wears black.

Evelyn.

I watched as he pulled the blouse over his toned body. They make me nervous. Everything about them does and I don't know how to act around them.

At first I'll admit it was scary but now in a way it feels comforting. I finally have someone. Or multiple people?

"So.." I began. "Where are we going again?" I heard him chuckle as I spoke ab it once more. "It's basically a ball with masks and you'll be fine darling you'll be by my side all night, okay?" He said in a little more stern voice. Like it was more of a demand.

I nod. He sat in-front of me on the floor his thumb ran over my cheek. "Darling, I really need you to listen tonight okay? There's a lot of dangerous people at this event and I can't afford to lose u."

My lips parted at what seemed like the most genuine thing he's said. It reminded me of Elijah's promise. Which confused me to why he was acting so harsh.

I nod. "I'll listen." A smile spread across his face. "That's my good girl." He kissed my forehead before going back over to a drawer and picking out a watch.

You could tell he had been working out, which adds up with Elijah being around me so much.

"Where is Elijah?" I asked out of curiosity. He turned around, his gaze almost empty. "Why? Do you not enjoy spending time with me?" My eyes widened as i quickly shook my head.

He smiled, walking over to his dresser he seemed to grab something, a file?

He walked over to me giving me it.

"What is this?" I asked as he walked to the bathroom. "I think it's good you know who your around."

Theodore.

I watched as she got comfortable on my bed. She's sitting on my bed. She has before she just didn't know, nor was conscious.

I know Elijah doesnt want to know, Elias doesn't really care. But she has to know and if you don't want her to leave tonight she should know it as-well.

I kept our younger cases out, mainly because those were a lot more how do you say that, brutal.

I dont want to scare her too much but she does need to know who's she's around. We're not nice people when it doesn't come to her.

Evelyn.

My lips parted seeing documents of murder, kidnapping, abuse. Everything you could possibly name. Theo was standing in-front of me with his awful grin again.

I moved back as he sat down on the bed. "No need to do all that bunny." He tilted his head holding out his hand. "I uh how do I know u wont hurt me?" I couldn't help but stutter over my words.

"Because when have i ever hurt u?" I looked down at my thigh swallowing harshly. His eyes turned soft.

"Evelyn baby, i didn't mean to hurt u with that I just.." he didn't know what to say. But he felt bad.

I got on my knees wrapping my arms around his neck. He wrapped his around my waist. "I'm sorry Evelyn, I don't want to hurt u." He kissed my shoulder. I nod. "It's okay."

"I know you didn't mean to." I smiled holding his face and before I could say anything else his lips crashed into mine landing us ontop of the papers.

For the first time I genuinely closed my eyes and let him kiss me. His tongue entered my mouth almost instantly. His hands dug into my waist holding onto my tightly.

"Enough play time for you two." I heard a voice and I almost jumped hiding under Theo who just tilted his head up. "Mind your business." He rolled his eyes before going back to kissing me.

I tightly shut my eyes knowing its Elijah.

"We have to go in 10." Theo groaned before getting up and taking my hand too.

"Uh is it possible for me to go back to my room and finish?" They both tilted their head. "Finish what?"

I knit my brows. "Uh myself?" A instant unexpected smirk on both their face

"we can do that for u too baby?" -Elijah

Masquerade.

E velyn.

"Do you remember what we told you, darling?" Elijah spoke from infront of me. i sat beside theo. elias across from him.

"yes." i nod i could see his jaw clench at me not calling him by the name he thinks i should.

"Good, i will go in with you." Elias smiled and i nod gulping. i looked up at theo who looked at me with a close to none expression-less face.

their masks were much more covered. their entire faces were, where as to mine it only covered my eyes and part of my nose.

i feel like that has something to do with the type of people they are.

i observed their clothes, i noticed they now put their guns in the back of their pants so i cant see it as easily.

they dont notice how much i watch them.

they must think im genuinely stupid...

~

My heart pounded in my chest I couldn't quite figure out why. All I could think about was the amount of people that were everywhere.

Elias held my hand, tightly. As if I could slip away any second — not that there was any way he would let that happen.

Everyone looked gorgeous. Their big luxurious dresses. Smiles on their faces. This is the most normal thing to them. Even Elias Elijah and Theo don't seem to feel frightened in the slightest.

I watched as Elijah and Theo walked upstairs and Elias held onto me walking behind them. He hasn't looked at me and I can't tell if that a good or bad thing.

We walked through a long hall way where Elijah greeted another person quickly before walking into a room that I couldn't see before due to it being as black as the wall itself.

The dark lights and mask down exactly help.

"You've made it!" I heard a loud chuckle before him and Elijah hugged and harshly hit each others back. I look up at Elias who looked at me with a odd smirk I couldn't exactly make out.

While Theo and Elijah greeted them. Elias bend down beside me. His lips almost pressed against my ear as he whispered something.

"I would suggest u watch what u do.. say. You remember my rule dont u sweetheart?" I nod gulping. They all gave me their own. Its hard to remember all but they pretty much align.

"Stay beside us at all times, I do not want to lose u out of sight for a second. If you have to go pee one of us comes with you for all I care I'll put my fingers in my ears if you're uncomfortable you are not leaving my sight Evelyn." - Elijah.

"As Elijah said, if you do leave our sight I'll kill everyone I find on my way to find you. Any deaths will be on your hands. We can decorate their graves together in the back yard, dear." - Elias.

"Just be good okay? I dont want to have to do anything unnecessary because you decide to tease or run. You belong to us. So please be good, doll." - Theo.

"Who might this be?" I came back to thoughts seeing as everyone was looking at me and all their masks were off.

"How rude of me, Evelyn." Elijah stood behind me bending down his shoulder placed on my shoulder. "Introduce yourself darling." His hands rested on my waist making me oddly frustrated.

"Uh" I looked at Elias who shook his head. They enjoy this. Making me intimidated.

"My name is Evelyn." I moved my hands to my mask. "Last rule, your not allowed to take that off darling." Elijah kissed my cheek.

He stood up and grabbed me by my waist sitting me down on his lap as he also sat down on the couch.

I gulped. They legit pull me around like a literal doll. I bit my lip looking at my dress. The soft fabric. It must've cost a fortune ...

Dont they somewhat care if they're willing to keep me this close to them?

"Arent you worried about her?"

"Why would I be? She knows. "

"Hm, alright."

I heard them continue whatever business conversation they were having. Something about oil land and other people. I looked at Theo who was clearly not bothered.

Elijah's hand was strapped around my waist like a seatbelt in a attraction park. I moved around seeing him talk I reached up to his ear to tell him I had to go pee.

He nod before letting me slide off his lap and giving Theo a sign to go with me. Theo held his hand out and I grabbed it just at the end of the hall there was a toilet.

"Why would u have to come if it's so close?" He chuckled. "Darling, are you serious?" I furrowed my brows. "That man in there, isnt getting out alive angel." My eyes widened.

"I don't understand they seemed so close and they're talking about business?" He smiled. "You know what they say 'keep your friends close and your enemies closer' there's a sense of truth in it." He opened the door to what looked like a private toilet. I could tell by the fancy space ship sound it made when the door opened.

"Rich people are extra." I shook my head. "I agree."

He ripped my dress down before turning around and putting his fingers in his ears. I think they're starting to notice I can't pee otherwise..

After I was done we we're ready to go but he didn't walk back into the room. "What would I need to do for a dance ma'am?" I couldn't help but smile at his silly personality coming through sometimes no matter how hard they try to be 'alpha man' whatever that means..

"You could start by asking for one." I smiled at his gasp. "Attitude, I see I see."

"Could I please have this dance?" I smiled nodding.

We walked down the stairs and as soon as his feet his the ground the people dancing made a path through the middle.

A little circle for us.

I always forget how much power they have around people because they don't take me to things like they often.

One of his hand went on my waist and one intertwined our fingers a little above our shoulder.

His feet moved swiftly I looked like an idiot trying to keep up. "You don't know how to dance?" He smirked. "I didn't get raised in a castle." I frowned.

"Me neither darling, here." He put my feet on top of his. My eyes widened at his clearly expensive shoes getting ruined.

"Your shoes are going to be ruined..."

"No shoes are worth as much as a dance with my lady." He smiled kissing me. It felt like a movie. Something every little girl dreamed of.

For a moment. We were normal.

Like stupid teenagers in love.

And I felt great.

Our fun.

E velyn.

I laughed as Theo drank himself into oblivion. We had since made it to the after party because he felt like Elijah and Elias took too long.

Not to mention he ripped off half my dress to be able to dance with me here.

I watched as the lights went from left to right. It didn't help that Theo looked better then ever. I couldn't quite figure out why I felt the way I did.

"Here." He offered me a drink and i stook it despite not being a alcohol person. I gulped it down in one go trying to become a bit looser.

But it only made me hornier.

I bit my lip kissing Theo who was clearly surprised, he slightly bend down putting his hand behind my head. He didn't dare pull away from the kiss he only deepened it.

His other hand wrapped around my neck somehow sending but-terflies down to my panties.

"Please." I whispered. His hot breath hit my face. "Hm? What was that?" He kissed my jaw down to my neck. I looked up my vision blurry. The red/purple lights moved everywhere.

There were easily over a hundred people and the only person I could focus on what him.

I squeezed my eyes shut "Please." Before I could even open them again he had thrown me over his shoulder it all went so quickly the first thing I saw was him towering over my in the back seat.

"You drive me fucking insane." He didn't hesitate for a second before ripping the top of my dress open and throwing the mask from my face.

My breath hitched as his hand went lower to my panties. I had never directly given them any consent. But now I was.

And all I could focus on what him touching me. As if fire was coming out of my skin and he was the water to cool me down.

He kissed me again, I wrapped my arms around his neck I could feel his hair on my forehead. I grabbed ahold of his hair with my left hand.

One of his arms was under my lower waist pulling me as close to him as he could. The other was playing around with my clit causing me to moan in his mouth.

"You're so fucking pretty." He kissed down to my breasts biting harsh bite marks into them I couldn't help but feel euphoria fill me.

A loud moan escaped my throat as he entered me with one of his fingers. "Ah Shh, that's nothing yet." He continued kissing, every-where.

he was marking me.

Biting in my shoulder, breast. He made sure his brothers would be able to see we didn't just go home. They were slowly getting more and more possessive.

I closed my eyes as he swirled his tongue around my nipple causing my stomach muscles to flex. Am I close?

How...

Theo.

I smirked looking into her wide green eyes. She has no idea what I gave her. She gulped ashamed. "Nothing to be ashamed of doll? You don't need to hide that I make u feel good."

She jumped hearing ticking on the window. The car had tinted windows so they couldn't see. I groaned rolling my eyes. I kissed her on her forehead before going to the front seat and letting her adjust herself.

I unlocked the door. "Took you fucking long enough." Elias stepped in beside me. "Hm" I cleared my throat looking at the back.

"Did something happen? Why is her dress torn off?" Before she could speak I smirked. "Oh something happened for sure."

~

"Why does it hurt?" She looked up at us from the bed. I look over at Elijah who has a gloss over his eyes. Obsession.

We all do. She knows what she does.

"Because your body is begging to be touched darling." Elijah spoke up. She knit her brows obviously confused.

Second person.

Elias went into the bathroom turning the hot shower on. In the other room Elijah and Theo were still having a blast playing around with her mind.

They both sat down on either side. One hand over her back the other over her thigh, neck, stomach.

She couldn't think, and before she came back to her senses her dress was gone leaving her in her underwear.

"Isn't she beautiful?" Theo whispered over her skin moving his lips along her neck. She could only bite her lip desperately trying to avoid any moans from coming out.

"Hm she is. Dont you want to have some fun baby?" Elijahs lips spoke against the side of her ear, his coldbreath sending a goosebumps down her skin. She shook her head knowing full well she wanted it too.

"Don't lie doll? Your body tells us enough." She gasped feeling Theo rip off the side of her panties along with the other side. "Sh, you're so sensitive, I love it." Elijah smirk against her skin making her squint her eyes shut.

"Lets go for a shower, dear." Elijah pushed her upFrom the bed making her open her eyes and walk towards the bathroom.

In excitement and fear.

Elias smiled watching her walk into the shower. She slightly covered her stomach but that didn't bother him. He could still perfectly See his name.

She slightly yelped feeling a body press up against her. "Relax doll." Theo's hands rested on her shoulders. They all enjoyed how sensitive she is to touch. Especially now.

She sucked in a big breath of air making Elijah chuckle. "Preparing yourself?" She realised she had no chance against any of them.

Not with how big they were anyways. She onlyReached till half their chest it intimidated her. And they loved it.

her eyes widened remember what Elijah and Elias had done earlier. She looked up at them in genuine terror and they could tell.

Elijah smashed his lips onto hers. Her hands pushed into his chest but it was no use as Elias grabbed ahold of them tying them onto a metal bar with a rope burning marks into ur skin.

Not to mention the hot water streaming down all their body.

She quickly gave into the kiss. She turned to Elias who picked her up by her waist lifting her onto him. A load groan escaped his lips. His fingers dug into her skin. Theo grabbed ahold of her neck making her kiss him Upside down.

While feeling Elijah circle his tongue around one nipple and play with the other. Not to mention Elias fucking into her relentlessly.

"Such a pretty little cunt." She moaned feeling a slap hit her clit followed by many more. "Plspls" was all she managed to get out between kisses and lack of air by Theo

She squeezed her eyes shut feeling another orgasm arise.

Theo let go of her neck. "Watch urself cum on my dick, darling." Elias rubbed his thumb over her clit overstimulating her even more.

Hot tears streamed down her face. The burning from the ropes the hot steaming shower. The euphoria she felt run through her whole body it was too much.

Not to mention. Theo and Elijah are biting and marking any inch of skin that was left unmarked.

"I cant please its too much" she begged. "But we know you better darling? I'll decide that hm?"

Fear and oddly excitement filled her body as he grabbed ahold of her hips and thrusted into her insanely harsh and fast. "I'm Sorry."

She begged. "You know we know your body better dont you?" Theo whispered into her ear she quicklyNod . "I'm gonna need you to tell us doll."

"Yes yes." She almost shouted feeling Elias finally Slow down she loudly Gasped for Air. "There we go. Wasnt so hard? Tell us how good of a fuck doll you are."

He smirked knowing full well he was embarrassing her.

"I'm im a good fuck toy for you" she spoke through moans, Elijah smiled. "You are? Whos fuck toy are you then?" She squeezed her eyes shut out of embarrassment.

A/n

Oh my god so many people have been reading this. I hope you enjoy it so far!! Makes me nervous that so many people are seeing this but thank u!

Aftermath.

E velyn.

    I opened my eyes yawning. By the light I could tell it was really late. Elias had his arms wrapped around me.

I sighed. I have to pee. I wiggled my way out of his arms slightly giggling when he grabbed ahold of Elijah who was laying very close to me too.

I walked to the door attempting to find the bathroom but the door wouldn't open. I sighed pulling on it harder. Is Theo there?

I shrugged heading towards the door I know theres a toilet not so far away. I peaked my head out not seeing any guards in the hall.

I made my way over to the bathroom. There's only doors here, I get that they don't feel at home...

I opened a door, cleaning stuff.. hm. Where was the toilet? I wondered around confused that there were no guards around until I felt my back harshly hit a wall behind me.

I flinched closing my eyes. "I don't think I need to ask."

I gulped realising it's Theo. I slowly opened my eyes. He only had black shorts on and a towel over his shoulder. I looked at him with big eyes. "Uh i was looking for the bathroom?"

"You have a bathroom." He deadpanned. He had some sort of dark undertone in his eyes that I couldn't make out what it meant. "Uh its locked i uh I just went to look for another." He furrowed his brows before seeming to get an idea.

In one swift motion he picked me up walking away from the room I was just in. Maybe he's talking me to the bathroom!

I looked at the floor as he carried me over his shoulder. I couldn't quite figure out where we were going but I hope there's a bathroom.

I heard a door unlock, and before I noticed he had thrown me on the bed. "You know, you keep trying to get away is really getting on my nerves." I gulped crawling back on the bed.

The smiling happy normal person he was a couple hours ago turned into a maniac.

"No I really wasn't I was looking for the ba-" I couldn't finish my sentence. "Evelyn." His tone was low dark. Which didn't help with the dark atmosphere.

"I'm not fucking joking around." I gulped at his tone. There wasn't more I could do with the rock in my throat and the tears streaming down my cheeks.

Out of all of them, he seemed the most normal. But the eyes he had the day he felt like he had caught me, were back.

Like pure evil.

He only came closer onto the bed and the only thing I could see was his figures and partially his eyes by the way he moved.

He crawled onto the bed making me fall off and try to go for the door.

Before I could open it my head got pushed against it sideways and his entire body pressed against mine trapping me between the door and himself.

"I'm really sorry I was really not trying to get away I don't want to make u angry." I cried trying to calm him down. "And going for the door is very fucking convincing isnt it?"

The only thing I could get out was gaps of air.

In that very moment I realised I had been delusional for trying to see a normal person in any of them.

His arms wrapped around me and he carried me over to the bed to lay down. "what about Elijah and Elias wont they wonder where I-" his hand covered my mouth just under my nose.

This doesnt exactly help my claustrophobia...

I closed my eyes until I heard a familiar sound of purring. Milo?

I smiled against his hand, which I doubt he felt with the snoring in my neck.

I softly left myself dose off feeling the cat lay against me.

~

"Why would they be so stupid?" Elijah chuckled at Elias's paranoid comment. "What if they find a way around. I think its time to move." He crossed one leg over the other. I had been sitting in Theo's lap.

We sat in what seemed like a library. The walls were white. Everything is actually. The couch the floor rhe carpet even most of the
books.

I looked down at my lap as they spoke. "Are you cold?" Theo asked
revering to my arms. I shook my head. "What is it with you and
lying?" He put a blanket over me.

"I want to move." Elias insisted. "What's wrong with this house?"
Theo spoke up finally inserting himself in the conversation "I don't
like this house." Elias deadpanned.

He's very quiet. With me he talks but around other ppl he shields
everything off I can tell.

"Is it possible for me to go to my room?" I asked carefully before
both their faces turned to me. I need to find a way out. "Evelyn,
darling. Will you come here?" Elijah moved his seat back and I sat on
hisLap as Theo let me go.

"Where were u this morning?" I know he knows. But he wants it
from me. His hand rested on my bare thigh. "I was with Theo." I
looked at his hand and his rings.

"Do you favour Theo, dear?" I looked up at him confused. A small
evil thought popped up in my head. I slowly nod.

Maybe if I make them hate each other they'll be busy with that
more then seeing if I escape?

"Hm." I could see his expression change but a small smirk appeared
on his face. "That's fine, we will just need to spend more time with
you." He caressed my cheek and my mental smile dropped.

Shit.

My eyes shifted between Elias and Elijah. "Uhh can i go to my room?" I asked in a panic Elijah knit his brows together.

"Why would u want that?" His thumb softly caressed over my leg and it was hard to concentrate. "I uh I need to do something." I smiled. "Care to explain?"

My eyes widened. "Shower.."

"Hm" was all he said before nodding and letting me off. "Ah, kiss first." I bit the inside of my cheek before quickly kissing his cheek.

"I'll take it." He smiled before letting me go off.

Elias.

I watched as she quickly walked off in Theodores shirt. I wish it was mine. She does still Have my bite mark in her neck. One of the only things I can focus on when looking at her. Including her lips.

"At the event I slipped her some viagra, I think it's still working." Theo smiled happy with himself. "Couldve told us, do you think she favours you?"

Elijah asked.

"I don't think so, she thinks were stupid. This is a trick brother." He chuckled. "Yesterday night she was crying I doubt she likes me the most right now." He can be a dick without noticing sometimes.

"I'm Going to Evelyn." I said getting off my chair and heading towards her room.

I knocked twice trying to give her as much privacy as I can. "Come in" i softly heard. I smiled to myself hearing her allow me in. For some reason I like her approval.

She was sitting on the floor looking at her dress. "Weren't you going to shower angel?" I sat down next to her. "I uh i don't understand how the shower works.." I chuckled. Elijah got the best most high tech machines around her room including her bathroom.

The door can also lock automatically.

Including her bedroom door and windows. Its quite cool.

"I'll help." I got up but she stopped me by putting her hand over mine. "Why me?"

I knit my brows. "What?"

"I don't understand." She looked down. "Dont understand what?" I asked. "Why you picked me?" I softly smiled.

"you feel familiar, like home." I smiled. Not that I know what a home is. I know she feels like it.

I got up turning the shower on. It has two big shower heads in the ceiling. The room really is huge almost as big as her bedroom.

I stepped out by my surprise she was naked my eyes widened. "What?" She said her eyes Also wide as if she did something wrong.

I shook my head. "No no nothing." Maybe she's getting comfortable? "Do you want to Join the shower?" She asked. I sighed remembering what Theo said. "I'm okay, you go shower."

a/n , thank u all for reading this book!! i did want to say ive been seeing a lot of SA comments etc, please remember this is a fantasy book and not reality. victim blame my character and youll be muted.

A game?

E lias.

　　I mentally smiled at Evelyn sitting between myLegs letting me dry off her hair. Elijah and Theo had been thinking about what to do with Victoria.

Or drinking themselves to death.

And there Elijah stumbled into the room reeking of alcohol. "I have a plan! We are definitely moving." I smirked.

"How did you get on that?" I said sarcastically. "Well if we move around so much people can't follow or anyways. We've been doing it for years so we will be doing it how we have been. And we don't have to worry about her i dealt with that." I knit my brows.

I assume he will tell me later. Not with Evelyn anyways. I think its best if we keep desth away from her with how she reacted in the past to violence. It doesn't work. She's very much a people pleaser.

But something is going on in her head that I can't quite figure out.

"Where did you learn to braid?" Evelyn asked I smiled. "Vic."

She nod. Theo or Elijah forced her to not mention vic anymore but she clearly misses a friend. I wish i could be that friend.

"Did she ever mention us?" I asked her out of curiosity. She made a short hm sound. "I don't remember I don't think so." Weird. I'm memorable?

"So she never said she had any siblings?" I asked again. "No I don't think so I really don't remember with all the drugs you guys have been feeding me." My eyes slightly widened at her comment.

She walked over to the mirror. "So pretty! Thank you." She smiled. She's acting off.

I stood up walking over to her. Her smile slowly faded and she backed up into the mirror. I stood in-front of her, inches away.

I like looking down into her big eyes. She looked away, but my hand forced her chin towards my face. Yet she refused to move her eyes towards me.

"Really?" I pressed the sharp edge of my knife against the right side of her waist. "You sure you want to do that gorgeous?" I couldn't help but smirk at her eyes immediately looking at me.

Pleading. Begging.

Begging to be carved? Or to be saved?

Surely not saved shes save with me.

I softly pressed the knife deeper. She only softly squealed, a panicked high sound. Her neck tightened her external and interior jugular veins showed perfectly.

I need to restrain myself Around her. Make sure I don't kill her, her pretty face is so tempting.

But I can't. Because I love her. And I need her alive to love me.

And Elijah and Theo, I guess.

"Ur not telling me to stop." I ran my thumb over her bottom lip. She let out a shaky breath. I took my knife back she loudly exhaled. Relieved.

Evelyn.

Elias's cold fingers ran over my waist. It didn't help that I was only wearing a top. His lips brushed against my ear. "I need you to listen okay?" My eyes widened.

I nod. "I've been, bored." His lips softly pressed a kiss against my neck. I couldn't help but feel my breath catch in my throat.

"I would like to play a game." I knit my brows still frozen from his hands trailing over my body. His other hand softly put a strands of my hair behind my ear.

"A game?" I asked. "Mhm, with you." His lips brushed against my ear once more whispering. "Are you up for a game with me, Angel?"

"What sort of game?" I asked interested. I hated myself for even being interested. Or aroused.

"You can run, and i find you." I knit my brows once more. His hand rested on my shoulder as he pushed himself back while looking into my eyes.

"How do I win?" He smirked. "I like your ambition. If you remain uncatched for 5 minutes." He smiled crossing his arms still standing dangerously close to my body.

"Five minutes?" That seems underestimating. Does he think it's that easy? I mean, I did practice with him before. "Fine but you don't get to use guards"

"Ofcourse sweetheart, that wouldn't be fair would it? Besides most are out for training." Five minutes.

"Okay what do I get if I win?" He smirked again. I hate it when they do that. That smug on their face like they already won.

"You decide." I cant even mention leaving, he will be upset. "Whatever I want?" He nod. "Anything?" Another nod.

"Hmm can I decide after I win." I couldn't help but smirk. Oh no. Am I picking up their trades?

He bow down a little his index finger under my chin making sure to lift it up. His nose was almost touching mine, millimetres away.

He just looked into my eyes for a moment before speaking. "Yes, baby." I hate it when they do that. Why does it make me feel weak in the knees.

"I'll play." This is my chance to get anything I want. Five minutes isn't that long? I should be able to do that. I crossed my arms ready for the battle.

"You seem quite confident." He stood straight his hands in his pockets. I shrugged "I think I'll be fine."

"We will see."

Let the games begin.

E velyn.

Okay all I have to do is make sure he can't find me. "You remember, no going outside. I will find you, if not in five minutes, in six. Seven. Or eight. I will find you Evelyn. Don't dare go outside." He made it clear I wasn't allowed outside.

Which I think is fare.

"I'll give you 30 seconds ahead." My eyes slightly widened. He underestimates me that much? "Isn't that less fun for you?" After all he's bored.

"What makes u think that?" Or it thrills him. "No reason. Lets start." I smiled.

I had black sweatpants on and a right black shirt, I need something I can comfortably move around in, not the doll dresses they put me in.

"You know your way out." He deadpanned. My heart dropped at his sudden change of demeanour.

I walked towards the door quickly. He gave me a thirty second head start. Which means I have about 20 left to get somewhere before my Time Goes in and he tries to find me.

Okay now don't get nervous. I need to focus. I'm so stupid. Ofcourse he's going to find me. Oh no.. I just realised I haven't even asked what he wants if he wins...

I'm so stupid. I ran as fast as I could pull my Legs up. There's no second floor in five minutes he will be in every room that's open he knows which ones are.

I quickly ran into the library.

Whenever I first came here milo was eating the bottom of the couch out and the stuffing. If I can just get in the couch he won't be able to find me?

I dove over the carpet under the bench. The hole was big enough to fit through but there was still too much filling.

Fuck.

"Come out my pretty little lamb." My heart skipped a bear hearing his voice. "No no." His voice echoes through all the halls. They all have very loud voices.

"Come out and play with meee" he teased. I hate him. I looked at a little gap in the wall between the book shells and the wall.

Its dark. I quickly ran over to the spot and sat between the shells and the wall.

My heart had never beat this fast. I dont even know what he wants if he wins. He can't win.

Surely a couple minutes have gone by?

I anxiously waited.

"Come out come out wherever you are~" he said walking into the library where I was. I could see his back. His tall muscular back. Not too muscular. But good enough to see in his sheer white shirt.

I stopped breathing, unaware.

"Hm, maybe I made a mistake after all." He turned around. He stopped for a second but walked on out and hummed on.

I waited until I couldn't hear him anymore. His humming and footsteps far in the distance.

I exhaled. "Am I going to make it?" I anxiously counted till five minutes.

Hearing the clock softly tick by helped aswel.

I slowly stepped out the dark.

Elias.

Its all going exactly as planned. I watched as she scribbled towards the door, I made sure she was covered incase anyone does see her though they're on strict orders to not engage with her anymore. I made sure of that.

Elijah and Theo have been busy, me too, just with a much more fun project.

I name it; getting Evelyn to love me back.

I will first make her happy by winning, she can do whatever she wants. She knows asking to Leave is not an option — right? She wouldn't be that stupid no.

I watched as thirty seconds had quickly ticked by. I chuckled seeing as I accidentally gave her 30 More.

I wonder where she is though.

What did she think was a spot I would miss. I am I fascinated by her. Not only how sure she is of this but also by the fire in her eyes when she does feel sure of something.

I walked through the hall. Don't get me wrong I love the fear in her eyes when I press a blade against her soft unmarked skin — only by me.

Its gorgeous. She perfect.that's why its time for her to realise she's not going anywhere.

"Come out my pretty little lamb." I chuckled to myself softly humming. I cant wait to see what she has in stock for me. Kitchen? I doubt she knows where that is.

I walked inside, the maids are in here cleaning, there's no way. Plus. They're too loyal to disobey bringing me this information; even if I told them not to.

"Mister Everest, is there anything I can do for you?" One of Theo's employees asked. She's always been nice. But I don't bother with their names. I only care for Evelyn's.

"No." I closed the doors again stepping out. What other room does she know, Elijah's office? Wouldnt be.

Ahh, the library.

I cant help but tease her. "Come out and play with meee."since i womt win I need some sort of entertainment.

I waited for a second infront of the great white doors. I can feel she's in there. Sense her.

Oh how she drives me insane.

"Come out come out wherever you are~" I walked into the library. I walked a few meters into the room, observed the curtains. The couch. In the corner of mt eyes there my little princess was.

Its cute, she has no idea I have a eye for this. After all my training, it's hard for me to miss anything.

I smirked. I did have more faith in her. She could've done better. I will train her, once I trust her fully.

I walked out again exhaling in euphoria. I cant wait to see what she does. I might be even more excited then she is. I looked at my watch. Only 1 more minute.

I cant wait to see what u have in stock for my sweetheart.

Was it so simple?

E velyn.

I woke up to a load knock on my door. I sat up almost instantly at the slamming noice. "May I come in!" A loud voice shouted in commando voice.

"Uh..." no?

I didn't reply and after a while he came in, "miss.. I have to escort you out of the building." My eyebrows furrowed. Out of the building? Why would he need to remove me from my own room.

I slightly giggled, my own room.

I sat up looking at the tall masculine male. "Mister Everest has send the request i do it myself." I shrugged. I only had my night gown on that Theo put on the other night.

I wonder how they'll react.

He instantly moved his face to the side not looking at me. "They have also suggested u put this on." (See picture above) he still didn't look at me handing me the clothes.

"I will be back once you're done miss." He stepped out of the room closing the door. I sighed putting on the outfit. Its a bit cold to be teasing in a night gown anyways...

I brushed my hair and also put that down. "May I come in?" He asked, somehow politely even tho his voice was very harsh and loud.

"Yes im all done." I Said putting my brush in my 'suit case' "I will bring u to the car, mister Everest has already arrived at the manner to assure your room to be to your liking." I nod grabbing my suit case.

"Oh no, give it here." He softly grabbed it out of my hand. He was around Elias's height not that they're not all very tall I can barely tell the difference.

"Come with me?" He reminded me when I zoned out I nod walking beside him. All the maids and staff, including guards were lined up against the wall.

"It's a thing out of respect." He noticed me looking around. "Respect?" I furrowed my brows. I would get it if they did it for Elijah and them but not me.

He didn't answer instead he walked me towards a big black car. "If you prefer you can sit in the back."

"Are you driving?" I asked he nod. "I'll sit in the front then."

"Why is it not someone who's driving like usually?" He softly chuckled before regaining his senses. "They don't like taking the risk."

He must be very dangerous if they think I'm safe with him...

"So who are you?" I asked as he started the engine and drove towards the gates. He also had and automatic button that made them Magically open.

"Well, I guess your bodyguard at this point." He looked infront of him, "my bodyguard? Why would I need that?" He shrugged. "You should ask your boyfriends that."

~ My eyes widened when we arrived to the... castle..

There was a parking space but no where near the entering. He took my bag out, he referring to my bodyguard?

I don't understand his function really and I don't know his name he won't tell me.

He pushed me forward making me walk to the front door, I shook my head. "Really? I don't think theyre going to be happy to have to come get you." He raised his brows in a just give up way?

I walked forward first under a couple bows made out of stone. "What is this..." he sighed. "A very very old building" I furrowed my brows. Yeah I can see that.

Outside Elias was smoking, he smiled his arms reached out and I hugged him, i dont know why. But i did. His warmth was somehow comforting..

His hand leaned on the back of my head the other around my waist as he flicked the joint away.

"Thank you. Lucious." I heard footsteps move past us inside. The big doors stayed open and Elias instructed me inside. I was met with a big blue floor carpet.

Two large stairs that crossed over each other.

~

I sat across from Elias who was smoking. I was glad the bubbles from the bath were high enough to cover my breast. His head rested against a little pillow on the service of the bath.

It was a fairy big bag so I don't really have a problem with sitting in it, along with Elias.

Elias suddenly moved closer to me, but just his face. Right in front of mine. My lips parted, I could feel my cheeks heat up.

Elias shotgunned the smoke into my mouth his eyes told me enough. I inhaled feeling the smoke slowly make my brain fuzzy. Along with the steaming hot bath.

"What do I need to do for you to enjoy being around us?" He suddenly asked. "I've tried everything. Harsh. Soft. What do u want?"

"I want to be alone." His jaw softly clenched not enough for someone who never saw him to notice.

"Fine." He looked away. I slightly furrowed my brows. "Fine?" He shrugged. "You can have ur own wing, I won't bother you, I'll make sure your completely left alone."

For some reason my heart shrunk a little. After some time, I hate to admit it. I liked how clingy they get. This must just be what anyone feels when they're forced to be around people....

I smiled "okay." He looked at me his expression with more anger. "If you attempt to leave, there's dogs on the property, before u get out you'll be attacked not by me, Theodore or Elijah. But a stupid dog." He grinned.

Sometimes I feel like he's genuinely insane.

"I won't leave..." a soft hum left his mouth, "then why do you want to be alone? What about being alone is attractive to you." His hair was wet, softly dripping drops onto his muscled tattooed chest.

"Well, i haven't had any alone time.." I looked at the bubbles. Not that I enjoy being alone. I just don't even know what it feels like anymore.

"Why do you want it." I shrugged. "I don't know Elias, I'm confused. This is confusing." I looked down. "I don't know what i feel or what I'm supposed to, you" I gulped.

"What?" He a-shed his joint and put it to the side. "You, you" i cant get the stupid words out of my mouth. "You touch me whenever you want you kiss me whenever you do, I want a choice. A real one because I'm not some object." I felt a tear go down my cheek.

He sighed. "I apologise if I hurt you Evelyn, I won't touch you ever again until you ask me to." I looked up at him. His eyes looked back at me softer.

He meant it?

"I would like to be left alone." Elias nod his head, "I can tell my love." He stood up I looked away a pink blush hitting my cheeks. Its so easy for him.

He got out and grabbed a towel. He wrapped it around his waist, in the door hall he spoke once more. "I'll leave you alone now, enjoy your time princess." My lips parted as I watched him walk away.

I feel relieved ..

Bit of a messy chapter but it makes sense with the next ones!!

West wing.

T heodore.

"What do you mean you told her we will leave her alone?" I angrily asked. This is bullshit. Just because Elias made a deal doesn't mean he can include me in his bullshit deal.

"She wants to be left alone." He calmly replied. Elijah seemed to be lost in thought. He didn't give much of a reaction instead he ate his breakfast.

"Make sure Lucious is around." Elijah commented.

"Oh right so she can go fuck him?" I said throwing my hands down on the table. "I will go see her if I want to you can't do anything about that." I sat back crossing my arms.

"Are you so sure of that? Little brother." Elias looked at me through his hair. "Yeah yeah little brother me all you want it's one year whatever." I rolled my eyes.

"You certainly are acting like a child right now, leave her alone, she will realise how much she misses us, especially in this cold old scary building." He smirked.

He does have a point. She's not going to enjoy being here and Lucious is only to bring food he won't do anything knowing Elijah would kill him without care.

This was the best place to be. Less likely to be attacked . She couldn't go anywhere. If she did try and leave. There's only one exit as we're on a cliff.

"Fine." I stood up walking out. "But I will say bye first." I closed the door harshly before walking towards the room I know he put her in before.

I opened the door and furrowed my brows when I didn't see her.

Ur fucking kidding me they moved her? I went back to the room Elijah and Elias was still eating. "Where is she I know u put her in the west wing." Elias shrugged and I walked over to him hitting my fist on the table.

"I get that u said bye, even tho its absurd. But I did not. I deserve to say bye to her." I said through my teeth. Elias looked at me with those expressionless eyes he's always had.

"Isn't it nice to introduce yourself first?" He said and I furrowed a brow. That's it. She's with the maids.

I smirked walking out happily figured it out. Walking down the stairs I saw one of the maids. Since it's a fucking castle we need those even tho I prefer not having them — only to clean my room duh.

"If you have any special things you like to eat I can tell the cheff." Melinda smiled. The only maid I really know here. Melinda sort of raised us as kids. Gave us chocolate bars even tho we werent allowed.

I stood against the hall opened watching as she nod and smiled at them explaining everything to her. Maybe she needs this. To be away from us to realise.

I looked down. "You should know better Theodore!" Melinda's voice ran through my head. I need to treat her better. Like her own person. Because she is... and not just my property.

Evelyn.

I nod smiling as the woman walked me down the old stone stairs. "So in this hall is everything we need, don't worry dear, you have plenty of time to do what u want to do!" She smiled warmly her cheeks puffed up and her eyes nearly disappeared.

I smiled "I would gladly help if there's anything I can help with." She grabbed ahold of my hand. Looked deeply in my eyes before saying "please don't, please focus on urself."

I nod before she excitedly walked towards girl dragging me behind her. "Lovely's I would like you all to meet Evelyn." She smiled proudly.

"Hi Evelyn!" I heard most of the girls say, some of them side eyed me some asked questions. "Is she working here now too? Oh we will be like sisters!" She squeeled with excitement that was quickly ripped away.

"No, Evelyn is an Everest" she smiled and my brows slightly nod before realising how I looked with the girls staring at me.

I could feel another set of eyes on me. I looked around until I saw Theo standing in the opening of the hall leaning against the wall.

His hand motions for me to come over. "Uh may I be excused?" I asked Melinda who held back a smile and waved me off.

Theo's arms wrapped around me pressing my body against his infront of each girl. "Excuse u darling?" He chuckled. "You don't work here." He held his hand out to take and i did. Seeing as he's acting somewhat normal.

We walked upstairs through a hall that led to what they call wings. There's five in total I believe. One for each of them and the maids. I don't know why they had another seeing as they don't have partners maybe for visits? Or vic...

He sat me down on the bed, I'll never get used to this. "We put all ur shampoo and stuff In the bathroom." He pointed towards the door.

I looked back at him as he held my hands. "Evelyn, I think you deserve an apology." He began. "We've treated you badly. Even tho I always meant it good and I know they did. U didn't feel good by it. I apologise." He didn't say what it was but it was clear to the both of us.

I smiled. "Thank you." I nod. I could tell he somehow understood and it did make me feel better despite still being locked up here because of them.

"I'll leave you alone now, doll." He grabbed ahold of the sides of my head and kissed my forehead before taking in my scent and getting up.

Leaving me alone.

I sighed. I wonder how many houses these people have. I know it might be hard for people to get. But I don't have anyone. I heard a knock at my door.

Elijah came in with milo. I smiled as the cat jumped onto my lap. "I thought you needed some sort of company." He rolled his sleeves up and he pulled his pants up before sitting at the edge of my bed.

"If you have questions, you can ask Lucious." He said looking at me through his hair. "Dont do anything stupid my dear. I am sorry." His thumb caressed over my cheek before he got up and left again.

I sighed looking at the closet I decided to explore. A desk with a pen and books. Closet with most of my clothes from my own home... half they obviously bought.

A little bench by the window. And a bathroom.

I looked at the bathroom, its clearly old but rich old? The stoned aren't falling down and the bath is shaped out of a big stone.

Before I noticed I sat back on the bed. There is no tv probably because it's really old. I laid back on the bed the purring of milo made me smile. His paws massaged into my stomach what I liked to call "making cookies."

I pet his head and he moved his hand against my hand harder eagered to be pet. "Just like your owners aren't you" I chuckled.

Do you guys like multiple POVs?

How many is tbe a max?

Dumbfounded.

E velyn.

   I haven't had much to do. Malinda told me I could help her clean around the house and I have until I fell down some of the stone stairs and bashes my leg open at the bottom. From then on she told me I wasn't allowed because they would be furious.

   I laid staring at the painted ceiling. Its been very cold especially in this stone old place.

   I put on one of the dresses that had been hung up in the closet. Lucious came by the same time he does everyday. "Miss?" He knocked on the door.

   I've told him he doesn't need to call me that but he shook his head. "You can come in." I said as I pulled my dress straight.

   "Finnley made you pancakes and uh yogurt and I think it's cranberry juice." He said as he brought the tray in that the maids usually would.

"Can you stay." I asked sitting on the edge of my bed where he parked the tray infront of me. It had little wheels under so it was easy to move thought he had to bend down to bring it.

He shrugged and sat on a chair on the other side of the room. "Do you know how they're doing.." I asked swinging my legs back and forth.

"Hm? Who?" He glanced at me. "You know... Elijah and Elias, Theo.." I looked at my food. "They've told me not to bring you any updates, saying 'if she doesn't want to see us she doesn't need to hear from us either'" he shrugged.

I rolled my eyes. They're so annoying. "You cant tell them I asked that." I deadpanned. He shrugged. "U cant." I furrowed my brows.

"I only have 1 boss miss you don't include within that." I sighed. "Fine then."

What am I going to do in this boring mansion with none of them around either. "Do you know if they're here?" I asked hesitant. Id like to go see them but not have them see me.

Just like sneak up to them and then leave?

"I believe Elijah and Elias were busy but Theo is somewhere around." I nod.

Before I finished my breakfast I told Lucious I would go and see if I could find Malinda.

Is it a good idea to go see him? I just got my space but I feel so oddly alone. Before I never had a problem with being alone because well I always was.

I stepped down the stone stairs. The first hall all the way to the left you can usually find her it's been a couple days now and I've found my way around the castle well.

"My dear! Goodmorning~" she sang happily as she saw me. I smiled. "Goodmorning Malinda, have you seen Theo today?" A small smirk landed on the corner of her lip.

"Yes he's near the library dear." She informed me and I nod smiling as a thank you. I walked towards the library which I don't think he is since she said near.

I've seen parts off the house but not all. I turned around as I walked into the hall there were paintings everywhere but hand painted onto the walls.

I flinched when I walked into a large hard body. "Oh I'm so sorry-" his hands caught me instantly putting me straight onto my feet again.

"You shouldn't be wondering around like that bunny." He grabbed my chin with his fingers. "I uh I was looking for you." My eyes widened at him walking towards me. I walked back until I eventually crashed into the hard stone wall.

"Looking for me?" I whispered down my neck. Oh my god. The butterflies in my stomach are killing me. He had a towel around his waist and was still panting from whatever he had done. Seeing as he was all wet he probably just worked out and showered.

"What can I do for my precious hm?" I blinked a couple times feeling myself get light headed. How is it that I only feel this around him... them..

"Uh n-nothing I just I just uh." I couldn't do anything but blink dumbfounded by his grip and the million butterflies going crazy inside my stomach.

He whispered "fuck" as he looked down, clearly trying to control himself he let go of my chin and stepped back from the wall. "It was nice seeing u for a moment, Evelyn." He gave me a small smile before walking through the hall again.

I stood against the wall dumbfounded.

~

"No dear what have I told u!" She scolded me. "But I want to help in some way." I said before handing the bucket of soap and the sponge back.

"That's not your responsibility, I appreciate it dearly but if they see harm on you, they won't like that." She said with a small smile.

"Here mother im all done." A boy stood by the door he looked in his early twenty's maybe 21/22 and around 5'9/11

"Oh yes thank u dear put your shoes over there so you don't walk the mud through the hole house." She pointed at a place for him to put them.

"I know mother I do this everyday remember." He smiled at her. "Oh my bad, this is my son, milo." She smiled. I furrowed my brows. Coincidentally?

That was until I heard a soft chuckle from Elijah who walked into the kitchen. "Nice to meet you milo, my name is Evelyn." I said trying to ignore Elijah who was standing against a drawer.

"How was rock picking milo?" He crossed his arms. As if I wasn't confused enough already, now i definitely was.

"Was good boss." He held his head up and stayed respectful. Elijah touched my shoulder but then let go. He clenched his jaw probably finding it hard to stay away as-well.

"Come on." Elias walked by Elijah who followed him as they went into the right hall. "So what do you do?" I asked curious about the rock picking.

"Oh i get a rope and I need to go down the cliff kick the rocks off onto the ground so the sea can splash over them." He explained in proudness.

"And does this have like an actual function?" I asked. "Yes Elijah is happy."

Theres clearly something going on with him and Elijah.

~ Elias.

I've been away from her for two days now. Two days. Forty-eight hours. 172800 seconds. 2/7th of a week. And all I can think about is her.

I sighed looking at my watch, 4:03 am. I cant say I completely stay away from her. Especially not now she's around that snob. I should remind Lucious he's the only person she's supposed to be around. Not alone with others.

I will remain 'calm' for now as Elijah puts it. My hand balls up into a fist when I remind myself of Theo teasing that he did see her. Apparently she needed something but didn't say what because she was like a dear in head lights as he put it.

Frightened.

I gulp thinking about my blade running over her soft skin, i wouldnt press it harsh not now. Not like I did with my name. Softly to let the small balls of blood fill up first. More like a scratch.

I felt myself go into a daze as I thought about it. Her thighs. Imagining her with tights on that show her skin just enough for me to softly press the tip of my knife in and rip apart.

I exhaled loudly trying to calm my thoughts. I need to able to be gone from her long enough that she comes to me.

Me. Me. Just come to me Angel?

I hope she comes back soon i dont know much longer I can get through this my Love.

Its taking painfully long.

I stood up from my desk. She's on the west wing. Mine is to the right of hers, north. The head.

I walked past her door. My head hit it softly not wanting to wake her. Knowing she's on the other side makes me feel safe. I smiled. A 5' little girl makes me feel safe?

Strange.

I shook my head walking away again. Space Elias she needs space. I walked out of her wing towards mine. I touched the door knob.

I'll go drive my motor for a little.

I feel for Elias <///3

Nothing gets me excited like, you.

E velyn.

    its been a week since i've seen them and i think it's time i let go of this. i looked into the mirror my hair still a little wet. i look a lot better.

less dead? drained?

I don't know but it feels good.

I wonder what it is that we have.. they say they love me and we are intimate but we've never spoken about it? have we?

I walked out into the bedroom I jumped grabbing onto my towel extra hard. "Oh m- im so-sorry" Lucious quickly turned around. "I didn't know u were getting dressed in here." He quickly ran out standing infront of the door outside. "Yeah not as if its my room." I mumbled.

I put on a simple sweater like dress. With how cold it is around here I should probably put some legs warmers on too. I decided to put my hair halfway upleaving some strands to fall in-front of my face.

I put my white sandals on and hopped down the stairs waiting to see Malinda. Instead i saw Elias. my eyes widened.

"uh.." i didnt exactly know what to say. he has black pants on with a black big hoodie covering his top body.

He pulled the joint out of his mouth before looking up at me and finally seeing me. He didn't say anything. He gave me the chance to, seeing as I wasn't going to he walked out right past me.

I gulped feeling his presence walk away. I think its time to let go of space. Each time I see one of them my heart misses feeling wanted?

The need they have somewhere it's reassuring.

I sighed.

"Yeah is your little stubborn act over?" Lucious chuckled leaning against the other side of the wall opposite of me. I turned around leaning on my side.

I rolled my eyes, "I don't know what I'm doing." I looked to the right. "How old are u?"

I was for some reason caught off by the question. "Why? Does it matter." I looked at him. "Not really, was just wondering. You somehow got them obsessed." He tilted his head poking his cheek slightly with his tongue.

I chuckled. "Yeah... it didn't exactly go that way." I looked down thinking about the night. The way Vic told me they are killers. That was my first impression.

"Hey, you okay?" He asked slightly tilting down to see the expression on my now looking down face. I looked up smiling. "I am, I was just thinking about something. I'm 19, but that doesn't say anything." He threw his hands up. "Never said it did." A small smile appeared on his face.

"What u smiling at." I furrowed my brows. "Nothing. Just thinking about something." He walked over to the cabinet, he got out a pot of peanut butter and another out of the fridge with jelly.

I observed as he made his sandwich and looked for my own opportunity for a little real freedom.

I softly tip toed off into the right hall. At the end there are two stairs and I know Elijah's is up somewhere in the right.

I should seriously make a map for this house.

I walked off into what seemed like ancient lights. I do think they're cute. They look like little lanterns. I wonder who lights them everyday..

"When did I tell you to do that?" I heard Elijah slightly shout, at least talk very loudly and harsh.

"N-no" a soft voice followed. "Then next time connect your two brain cells and think before you put rubbing alcohol over my leather seat."

I stood dumbfounded in my tracks as the girl ran outside and down the stairs past me. I could hear Theo chuckle.

I gulped, "do you see in what type of people they turn without you hm?"Lucious said as he ate his sandwich and leaned his back against the rails of the stairs.

I slightly jumped not hearing him or noticing his presence before. I looked at him. Almost in a questioning way. Maybe I needed someone to tell me to go talk to them. But he's been saying that in every way he can.

I looked ahead. At the few stairs that were covering myself from being seen by them.

I inhaled loudly as I heard Theo and Elijah talk. "Are they all there?" I looked back at Lucious who nod his head. I sighed. "Okay. You go." He chuckled. "Yeah yeah wouldn't wanna hear all the clapping." I furrowed my brows. Why would we be clapping...

I shook my head hearing Lucious walk down the stairs I began making my way up.

I took another deep breath in i dont know why — but I felt the need to prepare myself.

I have no idea what to say to them.

Elias.

I couldn't even begin to explain the overwhelming feeling I felt when I finally saw Evelyn light up my room again. I already wasn't busy with whatever they are talking about but now — now I don't hear anything.

I watched her grab ahold of her other hand and look down as she didn't know what to say. "So you've finally had enough?" Elijah leaned forward over his desk. She looked up at him. Her glass eyes. Her perfect beautiful eyes.

It may sound extreme, but if I ever can't have her. I'll make sure I can have her eyes. No one deserves to even be looked at by her.

By my angel.

She looked at me. My heart skipped a beat. I would say if I'm a teenager again but, my heart only beats with her around. Not before. Not this week — but now.

Its exploding.

Its overwhelming.

"U don't have to say anything Angel. Would u mind closing the door for me?" A small moment of fear going through her eyes. I smiled. I didn't know overwhelming could turn into excitement this quick.

Soft.

E velyn.

I looked down as I heard their conversation stop and I felt every pair of eyes on, me. "So you've finally had enough?" Elijah's eyes pierced through my skull.

I looked up at him. "U don't have to say anything Angel. Would u mind closing the door for me?" I felt a pit in my stomach. Almost as if it dropped.

I looked at the big brown door stopped by a big door stopper. I moved it aside and closed the door softly by the handle.

My heart beat fast, faster then I could keep up with. I turned around. They looked like they had been starved from emotion.

"Come, sit." He pointed over at the chair in-front. "How was your break, darling. Has it satisfied ur expectations?" He sat back eying me down.

Stupid come on talk. "She's so nervous she can't get a word out." I gulped feeling Theo behind me.

His breath hit the back of my back as he spoke next to my face. "I bet you must've had some tough moments alone, mm?" The rasp in his voice send a shiver down his spine. Almost as if I could feel it.

"I enjoyed, my alone time, but I also came to the conclusion that I may, uh." I looked down frantically fidgeting with my dress. "Well." I gulped.

"What is it darling? Spit it out." Elijah observed with full attention. Theo breathing cold air into my neck didn't help either. I inhaled deeply trying to regain my senses.

"I may have uh discovered that I may have a little sort of feeling for you." I looked down my heart could practically jump out of my chest and run away with how fast it was going.

"Just me darling? I don't think Theo or Elias will be very happy with that." He said in a fake sympathetic tone. He knows I didn't just mean him.

"You didn't like that night we fucked in the car doll?" I harshly swallowed again squinting my eyes closed. They love to torture me. "She's so easily flustered."

It terrified me that Elias hadn't said anything yet. Not a single word. It was just Theo and Elijah who were torturing me.

"I uh i like them too?" I questioned. "You don't know? That hurts my feelings bunny." He pouted and I looked at him. "Come on, tell me tell me." He chanted as a child while smiling at me.

"I like you too..." I bit my lip. For a second he had to regain his senses, but then he smiled at me again. Crazy. "I love you too miss

Everest." He sat down across from Elias again on the opposite side of the room.

"Oh, I failed to tell you. Elias rather talk to you alone when we are done. You see, Elias is a very loving person Evelyn, but you've pushed him away and even though he accepted that for you, he wasn't happy with it dear." I gulped looking at Elias who seemed to be acting completely, normal..

"Now tell me. Has Lucious behaved." I furrowed my brows. "Isn't he loyal to you." Elijah smiled. "He is, but he was supposed to take care of u in whatever way u needed, did he succeed, to you?"

He cares?

"Yes, he did." Elijah nod. "Well then, I wont kill him." My eyes widened. "Did any of the girls bother you?" I slightly tilted my head. "No? Why would they?" Elijah shrugged "no reason."

"That's a weird question. Why would u worry about that?" I asked curious. "No reason darling." I stood up bawling my hands into fists.

"If you want me to stay around you, all of you. I want you to tell me when I ask." I said annoyed. Elijah's expression wasn't phased. "I understand love." My eyes widened. Okay? Okay.

I sat down. "So?"

"Because I told them if they would I would make sure their tongue would fit their snake persona." Theo spoke up. My heart dropped. I don't even wanna know what that means.

"Still want to know everything?" I pressed my lips together unsure what to say.

Elijah stood up and so did Theo. I was confused for a second until I realised this was what he meant by Elias want to talk to me

He sat on the chair beside me. The one the girl apparently ruined. At first I was too scared to look into his eyes.

But after a while I couldn't resist. His deep passionate brown eyes stares back at me. Telling me everything he wanted to say.

"I like you too." I said softly. He smiled. His eyes slightly disappeared when he does. But not when he faked it. Its how I know its real.

"I love you more my precious." He held his hand out and I gave him mine. "I know this all went this quick for you. I hope you've had the chance to think about things so you don't ever have to make me go through something as excruciating as this my love." His hand tightly held onto mine. "I have, but I do need time to figure this out, whatever this is." He nod. "If you ever want help. I'm here beautiful."

"I just want to know what this is that you want?" He knit his brows slightly. "You?" I couldn't help but chuckle a bit. "And your okay having that with your brothers?" His face changed into a weirded out one.

"No, no that's not how this works.. we are in a relationship with you. And you with us but not us together..." he tried his best I nod my head. "I think I understand, I'll think about it."

"Did someone hurt you?" I furrowed my brows, no? No one.. I looked down at where he was looking. The side of my leg I scratched on the stairs a while ago. "No I was trying to help clean and I got clumsy.." I admitted embarrassed.

"Why were u cleaning? There people for that." I sighed. "Nothing."

His eye softened as if he was really trying to understand but couldn't grasp it. "It may sound odd to you, but I like to help people." I looked down. He smiled. "Ah, im sorry darling i was scared you felt like u needed to repay us." he smiled, his eyes pierced through my mind.

Sometimes I get scared he can read my mind.

"Now, do u want work?" My eyes widened at the question not because he said it because that would mean I would get to go out?

He patiently waited not taking his eyes off me. "Yes." I nod. His expression didn't change he is terrifying when he looks at me like this. As if he knows exactly what's going through my mind.

"What would u like to do?" He asked, interested. "Like barista?" I said. It sounds stupid compared to what they do. "Done." He held my hand.

My heart somehow fluttered. I could see some sort of spark go through his eyes.

Sorry I haven't been uploading much, I've been very busy. Hope u enjoy this chapter.

Memories.

E lias.

"Yes, I'm willing to pay the money, I want it by tomorrow, done for use." I spoke over the phone. "It will be done tomorrow youll just have to sign the papers."

"I will, pleasure doing business." I hung up the phone. "What did u do?" Theo asked as if I couldn't tell he had been standing there for 5 minutes. "How is that your business? U dont have to know everything." He furrowed his brows and his hands up into fists like he's done ever since we were kids. He's always been an aggressive little hot head.

"If it involves Evelyn it is my business." I smirked. "Ask her." Before he formed another thought in his empty nut shell he ran off to find Evelyn.

Evelyn.

I smiled watching as Milo (son of Malinda) planted a little plant on the edge of the cliff. He said it would glow they have them all over the property they lead out some sort of path.

"Now all it has to do is get comfortable before night and it should glow up." He grossed his arms smiling proud of himself. I couldn't help but laugh at his posture. "Hey u try plant with them nails." I gasped. "U think I can't plant a plant???"

"Of course not, especially not with them basically carrying u around on a satin little pillo-" he abruptly stopped, I realised why when a large hand turned me around by grappling my shoulder. "A word please?" He's trying...?

I nod. "I'll be right back milo." I waved before Theo pushed me forward out of sight of milo into his bedroom.

I don't remember if I've been here before. It looks like Theo's room tho. "What did u talk about with Elias?" He asked while glancing at my outfit.

"Just some things." I said hiding a small smile. He smirked. "Oh u think u are in control now? That's adorable." I closed my eyes feeling my back hit into the door and his hands on my waist.

My stomach for some reason fluttered, it has to stop betraying me. I shouldn't be enjoying his big hands on my waist..

"U have been depriving me for a week I would watch it if I were u. Now tell me doll, what. Did. U. Talk. About. Hm?" He pressed his knee between my legs causing a soft wimper to leave my mouth. "Come on make it easy for yourself?" My breath hitched.

"Just that i uh would like um a job.." I closed my eyes shut not wanting to see his face. His breathing stayed in my neck. I could tell he was taking it in, Theo is slow with new things especially when he can't do what he wants and the fact he can't do much more then this actually not even this drives him insane.

"A job? With us?" I shook my head softly. "Where? Where are u gonna have a job?" He asked slightly annoyed. "Uh well I wanted to do something as a barista.." he let go of me.

"A fucking barista? Ur worth so much more then that. What the fuck is he up to.." he turned around thinking. I took the chance to step out and walk away.

I felt empty headed I blinked a couple times before I ran into Elias. "Hey? Hey are u okay?" He grabbed ahold of my shoulders. All I could see was his chest before my eyes closed.

Elias.

I'm sorry. I grabbed ahold of her legs and one of my arms under her back. I'm sorry for this. Its a apart of getting them to understand ur freedom.

I carried her around to her wing, to her room. I gave her a credit card and a laptop to be able to order stuff. Since we will be here for a while. I laid her down in her fluffy white bed. I smiled at her face as she slept. I missed watching her sleep. I got up but sat down again as she mumbled something.

"Please, Don't go.." her eyes softly fluttered. I smiled kicking my shoes off and laying down beside her on-top of her bedding. She laid her little head on my check. I caressed her hair. I shortly shifted off to sleep too, it's been a long time since I've comfortably slept.

~

"No no no no-" she shouted before she sat up panting. "Baby? Calm down im here its okay?" She looked at me her eyes widened. "No!" She shouted. I furrowed my brows. "Are u okay?" She rubbed her eyes. Panting she realised she was awake.

"I uh im sorry.." she looked embarrassed. "It's okay, I used to have a lot of nightmares. Are u okay? Do u want to tell me what it's about?" She gulped I could tell by how hard she swallowed. It was about me or one of us. "I don't know." It definitely was.

"I wont judge u my love maybe I can help? To calm ur mind." I smiled holding my hand out. "I'm scared you'll be hurt." She looked at me her eyes watered.

"I wont be hurt darling. Go on." I ensured her. "In my dream you killed.. Victoria.." I sighed. She still cares about her. "Victoria is living her life somewhere,precious."

"Pinky promise?" ~

"Do you promise to never leave me brother? Theodore scares me..." I smiled at how much she trusted me. More then Elijah and definitely more then Theodore. "I pinky promise okay?" I smiled at her eyes lighting up. She quickly nod in excitement before she wrapped her pinky around mine. "Please never leave me.." her arms wrapped around my waist as she pressed her face against my chest.

"Elias?" I slightly shook my head. "I pinky promise." I wrapped my pinky around hers. How odd.

She smiled and kissed my cheek before getting out of bed into the bathroom. I stood up and walked towards my room.

I opened my drawer seeing the letters Vic has been trying to send me for years, with no answer. It saddens me from time to time.

I bet mother and father would've been proud of her.

I sighed. Stuffing them away under a note pad.

"What is on your mind?" Elijah spoke up. "Nothing." I turned to look at him. "I can tell, you're more quiet then usual, and you've been riling Theo up, why?" He crossed his arms.

"Theodore does that himself no? She asks to be stayed off and he can't." I shrugged. "U put that in her-" I cut him off.

"No I did not. Its normal for someone to not want people to just touch her, you should know that Elijah." I looked out at the window. "Do not." He slammed the door before walking off.

I shrugged. Does that count as riling up as well then?

Lightning Source UK Ltd.
Milton Keynes UK
UKHW010716160223
417123UK00005B/309